KU-750-142

AN UNCONVENTIONAL ACT

When Jenny Castle appears in Adam Prettyman's theatre barn one evening saying she has come to sort out his finances and look after his children, he knows he needs the help and is unable to refuse. Full of self-blame after the death of his wife, he wants only to lose himself on stage, the one place where he knows he is not a failure. But Jenny needs to hide too, from a man without humanity or soul who could bring down destruction on them all . . .

Books by Jan Jones
in the Linford Romance Library:

FAIRLIGHTS
AN ORDINARY GIFT
ONLY DANCING
A QUESTION OF THYME

JAN JONES

AN UNCONVENTIONAL ACT

A Newmarket Regency Novel

Complete and Unabridged

LINFORD
Leicester

First published in Great Britain in 2017

First Linford Edition
published 2019

Copyright © 2016 by Jan Jones
All rights reserved

A catalogue record for this book is available
from the British Library.

ISBN 978–1–4448–4098–8

BROMLEY AL
PUBLIC
LIBRARIES

CLASS
LPB/F

ACC
03074028

UL   1 2 APR 2019

Published by
F. A. Thorpe (Publishing)
Anstey, Leicestershire

Set by Words & Graphics Ltd.
Anstey, Leicestershire
Printed and bound in Great Britain by
T. J. International Ltd., Padstow, Cornwall

This book is printed on acid-free paper

AN UNCONVENTIONAL ACT

is dedicated to my lovely readers

You wanted a fourth Newmarket Regency
— here it is

1

Newmarket, Suffolk: June 1817

As the carriage rattled to a halt, Jenny felt an unexpected blaze of fire ready itself along her veins. If she could just get through the next five minutes, her constant vigilance would reduce from being crucial to merely advisable. After the events of the last month, even that small lessening of tension would be welcome.

She gripped her aunt's hand. 'Courage, Aunt Sophy. Remember, we are simply paying a call on your good friend Mrs Penfold, as we have done any number of times before. You will lean on my arm and we shall discourse normally as we walk up the path. Anyone watching will see nothing untoward, nothing untoward at all.'

Her aunt made a distressed movement. 'It will certainly be more pleasant residing with my dear Martha than it is at home now, but . . . Oh my love, are you sure you will not change your mind and stay also?'

Jenny shook her head resolutely. 'I dare not. I refuse to bring danger to you or our friends. Once away from Newmarket, I will disappear for four months until my inheritance comes in, and after that I shall be my own mistress and all will be well. You need not worry about me, dear aunt. Be sure I will keep in touch by circuitous means.'

'Your poor papa would be mortified to see you in these straits.'

'Hush. Papa and Mama are both now at peace, and considering their pain, I would not have it otherwise.'

'You will take care, my dear?'

Jenny kissed the faded, elderly cheek. 'The best care in the world. I am very fond of myself. Now remember, stay with Mrs Penfold, and admit my cousin when he visits — as he most surely will — but tell him I have departed. On no account return with him, no matter what plausible account he may manufacture of me or anyone else we know. Whatever he claims, it will not be true. It will be a ruse to put you in his power and to give him a lever to use against me. Take stout footmen with you whenever you go out. I would not put it beyond him to abduct you and Mrs Penfold both, merely as a conduit to me.'

'Oh, my dear . . . '

But it was time. The footman had run forward from Penfold Lodge to assist them with alighting and was even now opening the door to the carriage. Their maids followed them down the steps, fussing with skirts.

Jenny gave her arm to her aunt as they strolled into the house. Behind her, she heard the clip clop of carriage horse hooves as the coach made ready to turn through the archway into the Penfold Lodge yard. All was day-to-day normal.

Normal, that was, until the moment

when a second footman closed the front door against prying eyes. As soon as it was shut, Jenny picked up her skirts and ran for all she was worth down the servants' passage, through the kitchen and out into the courtyard. Willing hands boosted her into the back of a cart whose driver was having a loud altercation with the groom of her own carriage about which of them had the right of way through the archway. She burrowed down alongside two previously stashed valises, and was safely covered by sacking just as the cart driver won his argument and swung victoriously out into the road to plod towards The Bell at Kennet, where it was due to pick up feed.

Jenny lay on the wooden boards with her heart beating loud in her ears, her legs trembling and the smell of hessian in her nostrils. The dash had taken less than a minute — but at last she was free. Her ears strained to pick up the noise of any other vehicles travelling in their direction.

A voice sounded over the rhythmic plodding of the carthorse; calm, slow and untroubled. 'All well in the back there?'

'Yes thank you, Flood.'

'Bide safe then. You've got a fair walk ahead of you.'

Jenny closed her eyes and tried to relax. She would need the respite of the next thirty minutes. It was likely to be the last for some while. But it was difficult to be calm when the jolting of the cart amplified her anxiety about the task to come, and her mind insisted on playing over the events that had brought her to this pass, starting with the arrival of her cousin just a month before.

★   ★   ★

Six coaches had drawn up on the sweep, vast quantities of luggage were already being unstrapped, and there was a great deal of shouting and stamping of horses' hooves. Jenny's heart thumped at this disruption to her life of quiet mourning.

5

Her gaze leapt from vehicle to vehicle, trying to separate post-boys and the resident servants from her cousin's retinue.

'So unlucky an occurrence,' tutted Mr Tweedie, polishing his spectacles fit to wear away the glass. 'I would have expected far more time to settle your affairs than this. Why, it is not much more than four months since your poor father passed away. Who could have guessed at favourable winds from the West Indies at this season? Even His Majesty's packet cutters are very often delayed, let alone larger vessels such as your cousin's cargo ships. I am most put out, my dear.'

Jenny scarcely heard the elderly family solicitor, though he and Aunt Sophy stood next to her on the steps to welcome the 4th Earl of Harwood and his countess to their new estate. As soon as her father had died, she had moved her own furniture to the sound rooms in the Prior's House, but it was scarcely habitable even now, so she had continued to live at the Hall. The next few minutes would be unbearably painful, handing over possession of the only home she had ever known to an unknown cousin.

Out of the foremost coach stepped a tall man with the habit of command. He ignored the commotion behind him, brushed away the approaching footmen, and sauntered towards the house. There he stood, staring in a gloating, triumphant manner at the Hall.

Jenny swallowed. This must be Cousin Vincent. His clothes were well-made and unexceptional. He would have been considered handsome had his features not been harshened by long exposure to the Jamaican sun. He put a hand to his right thigh in what seemed to be a habitual gesture, and Jenny saw with a start that a whip of oiled leather nestled against his hip. She moistened her lips, trying to ignore her unease. 'Welcome to Rooke Hall, cousin.'

Light grey eyes, shocking against the swarthy face and dark hair, glanced at her, assessed her, dismissed her.

She continued, 'You must forgive us if we seem a little unready. We did not anticipate so early an arrival. You have had fair winds indeed to make such a swift passage across the Atlantic. I trust the voyage was pleasant?'

'I noticed no inconvenience.'

His voice was cool and remote. Jenny looked beyond him at the coaches, overcoming her first startled impression at seeing dark-skinned servants emerging from them. Her cousin's family had lived for three generations in the West Indies. Naturally his household would not be the same as hers. But not all the faces were foreign. A pallid, fair-haired child in blue velvet knickerbockers had been set down on the gravel sweep, his hand tightly clutching that of a buxom African woman. This must be Eddie, Cousin Vincent's son, six years of age according to the notice they had received on the occasion of his birth. Jenny's heart softened.

'Which carriage is Lady Harwood in, please?' she asked. 'I should very much like to welcome her to her new home.'

Again that cold voice. 'My wife passed away on board ship. She was not strong, and the rigours of the passage did not agree with her constitution.'

Jenny gasped. 'How . . . how dreadful! My sincere condolences.'

Cousin Vincent made no acknowledgement of her sympathy. His attention was still on the Hall. The greed of acquisition was writ plain on his face and in his bearing. The contrast to her gentle, scholarly father, who had worn his earldom so lightly, could not be more marked. A prickle of fear and dread ran up Jenny's spine.

2

Clare, Suffolk

The office at the end of the barn was dark, the pool of light from the lantern on the crowded desk the only illumination. Adam stared hopelessly at the jumbled ledger and the pile of unpaid accounts. He scrubbed a hand over his eyes. The longer he failed to deal with this mess, the worse it grew. Mary would have sorted it out in half a day. No, he corrected himself savagely, Mary would not have let it get this bad in the first place.

Behind him — behind the makeshift partition and the screened-off dressing rooms — the stage slept. He wished it were otherwise. Wished it were two hours ago when he, Adam Prettyman, actor-manager of the Chartwell Players, was lost in *Hamlet* for the gratification of the audience. He would rather play the most difficult role in his repertoire seven nights a week than deal with business matters.

There was a sound. A tiny throat-clearing from the doorway. Adam looked up out of the yellow light, towards where a thicker shadow than the rest resolved itself into the shape of a woman. She was small, dressed in a good travelling cloak, with soft brown hair escaping from the confines of a plain bun. A stranger.

'I came to ask a boon, but I think you are in trouble yourself,' she said in a wry, compassionate voice. 'Will you allow me to help you?'

Adam's lip curled. What was it about actors that made them so desirable? He spoke roughly. 'Why yes, if you can conjure money for the farrier from a column of deficits. You have mistaken your path, madam. The theatre has closed for the night. There is no business for you here. I suggest you go home.'

11

The woman came forward into the light, drawing off her glove and proffering a hand. There was a bone-deep tautness to her that she was endeavouring not to show. 'I have always found the problem with minus sums is that it does not do to put too many of them in the same place. They are over-apt to crowd together and produce an atmosphere of unwarranted gloom. You are Mr Prettyman, I take it? I am . . . ' She paused, and a sudden smile lit her eyes. 'I am Jenny Castle. I fancy it will be rather liberating.'

Her composure in the face of his rebuff was unexpected enough to jolt Adam out of the bear cage of his thoughts. He found himself taking her hand. Her skin felt soft and delicate, alien to his touch. He dropped it as if burnt. 'Have we met? I do not . . . '

She chuckled. 'My friend Susanna Kydd said the Chartwell Players were just what I needed — and that I was just what you needed.' She glanced at the ledger and her eyebrows rose. 'In

12

which belief she was entirely right. You appear to have allowed these figures to get dreadfully unruly.'

No one had chuckled in Adam's presence since Mary had died. Already off balance by the visitor, the sound dropped a spark on the debris blowing about in his soul. He glanced at the page. 'There did not seem any way of stopping them. You are acquainted with Mrs Kydd?'

'I am, and indeed, I am here by her commendation. Do you have lodgings in the town? I have my luggage with me. It is astonishing what one can fit into a couple of valises when one only has the two hands to carry them. I was quite surprised.'

Luggage? Lodgings? Who was this woman? He gathered his wits. 'Miss Castle, I — '

'Jenny,' she said firmly. 'I think you must call me Jenny. A relation, perhaps. Bestowed upon you for the summer to take care of your books.'

Adam began to wonder if someone

had been dosing his ale. 'I have no relations. The whole company knows it.' He broke off. 'Listen to me. My brain must be disordered. I am talking as if what you say makes sense. I do not know you. I do not know what you are doing here. Pray, go about your business and leave me alone. I have enough concerns without you adding to them.'

To his discomfort, the woman tilted her head, considering him. 'What is your most pressing need?' she asked.

He gave a bitter laugh. His most pressing need was to wind the clock back three years to a time when Mary was well, the Chartwell Players were in funds, and the only cloud in his sky was whether Ann Furnell would remember her lines that night or not. 'Five shillings and ninepence for the farrier,' he said flippantly.

She opened the drawstrings of her reticule. For all her composure, he noticed that her fingers were not quite steady. 'Here are ten shillings,' she said, counting a pile of silver onto the desk. 'I make you a present of them. Mr Prettyman, I badly need a place to stay. A place where I may be busy and useful and where no one will remark upon me.'

Adam's eyes were drawn to the shining coins. Coins that were no part of the takings. Coins he didn't have to divide among the company so that they too could pay the farrier or the butcher or the surgeon. He bolstered his willpower, raised his head to refuse, and met the desperate honesty in her gaze. His mouth acquired words of its own accord. 'If I am to call you Jenny, you had best address me as Adam, not Mr Prettyman.'

The woman — Jenny — closed her eyes briefly. 'Thank you,' she said in a heartfelt voice. 'Thank you very much. I will do my utmost that you might not regret your decision. Where do you stay? Susanna mentioned you had children.'

'I . . . yes. Lottie is no doubt with

Mrs Jackson and the women. I do not know where Will is.'

'Permanently? Or just at this moment?'

He felt the tiniest pin-prick of amusement at her response. 'After the performances, his time is his own. I am best left to myself when wrestling with money matters, and he knows it. He usually slides back here to sleep.'

'Here?' Jenny appropriated the lantern and swung it around, locating bedrolls, assessing the floor space with a tiny vertical wrinkle between her eyebrows.

Adam watched her, diverted despite the preposterousness of the situation. Who *was* this Jenny Castle? Why had their friend Susanna sent her to him? If she needed somewhere to stay, why was she not at Kydd Court with Susanna herself?

'In general, all those of my company who do not have coin for an inn bed down in the theatre together,' he explained. 'Or there are the wagons, if you would prefer privacy.'

'I should *prefer* to be with the rest of

16

you.' That was said in a very decided manner. 'But I did not think to pack sheets or a blanket. How foolish of me.'

'It might have been difficult, with only two valises.'

'I daresay I could have contrived some way of . . . ' She paused, her eyes widening. 'Are you teasing me?'

Adam was startled. Was he? He thought he had forgotten how. He had not been so disconcerted for years. 'I was sympathising. You may rest easy. I have extra bedding.'

'Thank you. I am sorry. I will try to solve more problems than I create.'

She was creating them already. 'Are you hungry?' he asked, taking refuge in the ordinary, the everyday.

She chuckled again. 'I confess I am. I would make a poor heroine, would I not? Your heroines on stage swoon dramatically or hitch up their skirts and escape when faced with adversity. None of them stand there pathetically with their stomachs growling.'

Amazingly, Adam felt his spirits

lighten further. He put his hand under her elbow to guide her outside. 'You had best meet Mrs Jackson. I hope you like chicken broth.'

'I am very fond of it. Who is Mrs Jackson, please?'

'Our senior female performer. She and her family have been with the Chartwell Players since Mary and I formed the company out of the ruins of a previous one. We'd not been with them long when the manager absconded with the takings, so we decided to set up on our own. Do not let Mrs Jackson's abrupt manner concern you. It conceals a kind heart. She was goodness itself with Lottie when Mary died, and will accept you without question when she hears you are Susanna's friend.'

He felt Jenny's arm tense against his palm. 'If you do not object,' she said slowly, 'it would be very much better for me to be a family connection rather than a chance-come friend. I can mind children as well as disentangle ledgers, if that would make me more acceptable.

Please, Adam? It would aid matters considerably.'

He stared. Why should such a prosaic person need to pretend she was not who she was? How could anyone as clearly sensible as Jenny Castle find herself in this pass? 'Mary's family disowned her when she left with me, so she has never talked to the company about them,' he said at last. 'Pretending to be her long-lost cousin should be safe enough. Tell me, why am I agreeing to this?'

'Because you need a bookkeeper.'

'Assuredly. And?'

'Because you trust Susanna Kydd.'

'With my life. And?'

She hesitated. 'Because my own cousin — sadly *not* long-lost — is trying to kill me.'

For a moment, Adam couldn't place the rolling sensation under his ribs. Then he realised he was laughing. Laughing! He had barely even managed a *smile* off stage for months. He was overwhelmed by the strangeness of it after so long, disoriented by the inexpressible joy which sudden, unforced laughter brings. And this composed, candid-yet-private young woman had caused it. But she *was* funny, and his chest ached with disuse. 'No, really, this is what I work with night after night,' he said, dabbing at his eyes. 'You cannot gammon me with such a tale, but if you are so desperate not to tell your secret that you must needs resort to melodrama, I shall not press you. Come, let me introduce you to the company.'

★ ★ ★

Permission to stay. Jenny didn't know when she had been so grateful and relieved, though in truth, she had felt safe ever since she'd slipped around the office door and seen Adam Prettyman's large, comely frame silhouetted against the lantern's light. She studied him covertly as she accompanied him out of the barn. He was a few years over thirty, she judged, fair-haired with intelligent eyes. It was strange to be

walking beside him instead of appreci-
ating his skill on stage. She smiled to
see his ribs still heaving. Laughter
suited him much better than the abject
despair she had walked in on. It seemed
she had at least got something right in
this fantastical situation. Would that it
might continue. He may choose to
disbelieve her, but for the next four
months she was playing for her life.

It was true dusk now, and too dark to
see the field and the wagons clearly, for
which she was grateful, having become
somewhat travel-stained in the sixteen
miles from Newmarket to Clare. But as
they walked towards where wavering
heat from the cooking fire was distort-
ing the late evening air, there was no
mistaking the massive upright woman
presiding over both it and the group
around her.

Mrs Jackson. Jenny recognised her
now. She had seen her as queens and
duchesses and formidable aunts a
number of times during the Chartwell
Players' visits to Newmarket. It seemed

it wasn't only on the boards that she played the matriarch.

And like any matriarch, she sensed a stranger before they were within twenty feet of her. 'Who's this?' she asked, looking at Adam.

Jenny moistened her lips. She had come to the next barrier, and this one required dissembling. She hoped she could manage it. 'My name is Jenny Castle. I am — I was — a relative of Mary Prettyman.'

A ripple ran round the group. 'Mary never mentioned family,' said Mrs Jackson.

'I can understand that,' said Jenny in a troubled voice. 'She was treated very badly. I often felt it so. I have asked Mr Prettyman whether I can travel with you for a while. To make reparation in a small way.'

'Are you an actress?' asked one of the younger women, her eyes flashing in the firelight.

'No,' said Jenny. 'I am a bookkeeper. I can figure accounts, mind children and do my share of the work.'

'I don't need minding,' piped up a youngster of seven or eight years. This was presumably Adam's daughter. She wriggled to the front of the group and slipped her hand into Adam's. He ruffled her hair, his face softening.

And with that one gesture, Jenny's desperate plan started to unravel faster than her attempt as a four-year-old to knit a stocking bandage for her pony. What was she *doing*, using these people? She straightened her spine, dispatched her qualms firmly back to the closet, and reminded herself that she would be giving the company a good return for their unwitting aid. 'You must be Lottie,' she said. 'If you do not need minding, perhaps I could teach you to draw, or help you with your sums.'

The girl's dark eyes studied her curiously. 'Do you know any stories?'

Jenny smiled. 'Yes, lots. And I have brought my favourite picture book with me, full of tales of ancient gods and goddesses.'

Mrs Jackson was not so easily won over. 'Vastly pretty, but it's late in the day to be making amends for your family.'

'I know, and I am sorry for it. It was not in my power to do anything sooner.'

'Jenny's been three days on the journey,' said Adam in a tone of finality, proving that he could act off the stage as well as on it. 'I've said she can stay and welcome, so be a Christian and ladle the girl a bowl of broth. I'll have some too, if I may.'

'Without being reminded? There's a miracle.' Mrs Jackson's gaze settled back on Jenny. 'What's your father about, letting you travel alone?'

'I am four-and-twenty, ma'am. My father, alas, is dead.' Strain and tiredness and an ache of grief that remained even after five months meant she did not have to counterfeit the tears filling her eyes. 'I have nowhere else to go.'

Whether it was the tears or the unplanned desolation in her voice,

Jenny didn't know, but the atmosphere changed perceptibly. A bench was shifted, space made for her and Adam to sit down with Lottie between them, and a thick slice of bread and a bowl of broth produced for each. After the day's fraught journey, her eyes constantly looking over her shoulder for pursuit, her ears ever on the alert for shouts raising the alarm, Jenny fell on the meal gratefully. Never had a simple soup tasted so wonderful. She said so.

'Good to see a young woman with an appetite,' was Mrs Jackson's only comment, but she sounded pleased.

The talk turned back to its previous thread. Jenny concentrated on her broth, glad to retire into the shadows. The main topic, it seemed, was a new play and whether Miss Lucy Jackson (the flashing-eyed damsel) could induce her mama to provide a fresh dress for it. 'For a princess would wear satin and lace in the newest fashion, would she not? A princess would not be seen in the same blue gown that Ophelia was laid to her tomb in, or that Melusine wore when she eloped to Scotland and got caught by Baron Fearsome on the way.'

'We can add a trimming,' said Mrs Jackson. 'Princesses have a deal more in the way of pin money than you, missy.'

'I don't have *any* money,' returned Lucy hotly. 'You and Papa always take my share. I'm sure the prince would like to see me in a new dress, wouldn't he, Adam?' She slanted a look up at the actor-manager through long, thick lashes.

But Adam's attention was on Lottie, whispering busily in his ear. His absent answer that a competent actress's playing outshines her costume did not seem to find favour with either mother or daughter.

Jenny accepted another thick slice of bread from a soft-footed African player. 'Thank you,' she said with a smile.

Adam's seemingly abstracted attention focused sharply on her. Too late, she realised she should have shown some surprise at the sight of a dark face. She dropped her gaze to her bowl. It seemed she had a lot to learn regarding everyday deception.

3

The evening did not go on much longer, for which Jenny was grateful. The fire was extinguished and the company moved in clumps back to the barn. To the *theatre*, she corrected herself. Lucy and Mrs Jackson had got either side of Adam and were talking earnestly at him, leaving Lottie to dance ahead with Jenny. The little girl had taken to her and seemed to have vast reserves of energy. If Jenny could have concentrated on more than one word in every four, it would no doubt have been invaluable, for Lottie chattered about the Chartwell Players all the way to the office, where she dragged out the bedrolls and then, looking blithely up at her, said she expected Jenny was too tired to brush out and re-plait her hair and it didn't matter at all.

But Jenny knew better than to let her

28

get away with this. It would have destroyed her credibility as being able to manage children. 'That's very thoughtful, but as you are being so kind to me, the least I can do is make you tidy for the night so the angels will see you are good and deserve to have your prayers answered.'

Lottie giggled philosophically and fetched out her comb and ribbons. 'And when you have done mine I shall do yours,' she informed her, 'just like I did for Mama.' Her voice wobbled. 'The others don't like me doing it for them.'

Jenny's heart was wrung. 'I shall be very grateful, for it is a most difficult thing to manage for oneself. But I warn you, my hair has a terrible tendency to slither out of whatever restraint is placed on it.'

With enthusiastic determination and not too much pain on Jenny's part, Lottie was doing very well when Adam walked in on them. The colour drained from his face. For a moment it was as if he couldn't speak.

Just like I did for Mama.

The sentence darted into Jenny's head. She nearly cried out in sympathy. What a dreadful blunder! No doubt Adam had often witnessed just such a tableau in happier times. She opened her mouth to say something. Anything.

'Papa,' said Lottie, 'Jenny needs a bed.'

'Yes, I was just coming to — '

'Next to mine,' went on the determined voice. 'Then if I wake up and . . . and she is missing anyone, we could hold hands, couldn't we?'

'Sweetheart, that's a lovely idea, but — '

But Jenny had heard the first 'I' and she had also felt the small hands tighten on her braids. 'I own that would be most comforting.'

'You would not prefer to be with the other women? I do not know exactly how they arrange themselves, but — '

'Papa, Grace *snores*. And Jenny wants to be in here with us.'

She jumped with alarm. *In here?* And

30

with us? This was an intimacy she hadn't bargained for. She controlled her voice with an effort. 'I understood you to say everyone slept in the theatre together.'

Adam gave a short laugh. 'A manager has few privileges. One at least is privacy for my family when it can be had. We use the office. The Jacksons and the Furnells have the dressing rooms. The rest bed down on the stage or push benches together in the pit as it suits them.'

Jenny gulped. When Susanna Kydd had described her former existence as a touring player, she had skimmed over the prosaic realities. It looked as if Jenny was going to be encountering them fast. 'Well, it will be most agreeable having Lottie so close during the night,' she said briskly. 'And it will not be improper being in here together, for we shall be well chaperoned.'

'If you are concerned about impropriety, you should not have chosen a company of comedians to travel with,' said Adam cryptically. 'But as you have, I shall fetch the spare blanket. And then I shall stay outside until you are ready and warn Will to do likewise.'

Even so, he did not look happy. Neither, to be strictly honest, was she.

★ ★ ★

In the event, Jenny didn't hear Adam and his son come to bed. She fell asleep the moment she closed her eyes. Such a steep plunge into an abyss of exhaustion could not be sustained, however, and she woke in the pre-dawn hours cold and acutely uncomfortable.

Lottie had been correct in her declaration that one of the young women in the company snored. Not only one. Lying in the darkness with her neck becoming stiffer by the minute and what must be a prodigious bruise developing on her right hip from contact with the ground, Jenny counted some half-dozen differently pitched snores from varying parts of the theatre. She shifted, listening to the untroubled breathing rhythms of Adam's family. How could they sleep so soundly when the straw pallets barely cushioned the floor? And how could she not have noticed that her pillow appeared to be stuffed with sawdust rather than feathers?

She corrected herself. There was one feather, for it had pierced the linen and was sticking into her temple.

She eased around until she lay on her back and promptly encountered another difficulty. She needed to relieve herself. At home, this would not have been a problem. There would have been a chamber pot under the bed. Here, as Lottie had considerately shown her earlier, there was a pail outside.

For all of two minutes Jenny weighed the likelihood of her lasting the night against the inconvenience of creeping outside now. The feather shaft and a particularly recalcitrant wedge of bunched straw convinced her. She slid out from her blanket, groped for her shawl and felt her way to the door.

The grass was scratchy underfoot. Jenny edged around the side of the barn, resolving that another time she would remember to don shoes before venturing out. The relief on finding and using the pail, however, was tremendous. She thought she had never fully appreciated the conveniences of her home before this moment.

On her way back, she stumbled over a dark bundle on the ground. She almost shrieked aloud as the bundle reared up.

'Take care, miss. It's rutted that way.'

It was Samuel Obidah, the African. Jenny felt ashamed of her instinctive reaction. It was the unfamiliarity of the situation, that was all, and a dark-skinned person on a dark night making it impossible to see him. 'Samuel,' she said in a low voice, 'I beg your pardon. I did not notice you there. Why do you sleep outside?'

There was a soft laugh. 'It's quieter out here.'

Jenny remembered all the snoring

indoors. 'There is that,' she agreed.

'And I like the space.' He lay down again, perfectly content. 'No walls to put a shackle on my soul.'

Jenny pondered the words and their implications as she crept back inside to the office. Given certain recent experiences of her own, she suspected she knew only too well to what Samuel might be alluding. There were worse things in life, after all, than an uncomfortable bed. On which chastening reflection the sole of her right foot was assaulted by a searing pain. 'Aaah,' she gasped.

'What is it? What's amiss?' Adam's voice was alert.

In the midst of her discomfort, Jenny took in that he was a man accustomed to nocturnal awakenings.

'Nothing. Ow. A splinter, I think.' She faltered, wobbling on one leg, unable to think what to do first. The pain was extraordinary. She needed to lean on something. Oh, if only she could *see*.

There was movement in the darkness. A large shape crossing to the desk. The sound of tinder striking. A candle flame blossomed into life.

'Sit down,' said Adam.

Thank goodness. Jenny sank gratefully onto the tall stool. Now she would be able to see what she had done.

But Adam had moved the candle to the floor and taken her foot in his hands.

'What are you doing?' she said in a whispered shriek.

'Extracting the splinter,' he said. 'Keep still and stop fussing. An injured foot on one person slows everybody when we travel.'

'Oh. Yes, of course. Very practical.' How stupid of her. Naturally he would not be making advances. His wife was only a few months in the grave and Jenny had the evidence of his dealings with Lucy Jackson to see that he was not the sort of man to take easy comfort. It was a little humiliating that he'd felt the need to explain.

'It is necessary to be practical when your living relies on sound limbs to carry you from place to place,' he said. 'You should have been wearing shoes.'

Simple enough for him to say. He wasn't the one who had embarked on the travelling life a mere eighteen hours before. 'I realise that now,' she snapped. 'I am not used to this.'

'Nor was I at first. One becomes accustomed. Ah, good, it's a large one.'

'Pray do not concern yourself with making me feel better,' she said.

He glanced up. Was that a flicker of humour in his eyes? 'A large fragment is easier to remove in poor light.'

'That is certainly one way of looking at it. How are you going to . . . ?'

But he already was. He had opened a drawer in a large travelling chest, unrolled a clinking length of material, and was searching along the pockets. 'Mary was always prepared,' he said. He took hold of her foot again in gentle hands and, with immense relief, Jenny felt the pain in her sole vanish. She twitched as he brushed his thumb across it, felt the warmth of the flame as he turned her foot to the light. 'I think that's clear, now.' He dipped a cloth in the ewer of water and rubbed it over the puncture.

Jenny jumped. The water was cold.

Adam took a small bottle from the desk. 'This will sting a little,' he observed.

'Aaah!' She bit off the exclamation. 'What is that?' she asked, her nose wrinkling.

'Lavender in vinegar. Mary was a doctor's daughter. If she had been a son, she would have followed her father into his profession and been made welcome. Being female, so many barriers were put in her way that she felt there was no place for her. She became an actress instead and enriched us with her gifts in both spheres. She had remedies for everything.' He paused. 'Everything except herself.'

'I'm sorry.' Jenny dropped her voice in sympathy. 'How long have you been without her?'

For a moment, she thought he wasn't

going to answer. Then, 'Since February,' he said on a sigh. 'The coldest night of the winter, but Mary was burning up. She looked at me, told me to carry on, then slipped away. Such a difference a moment makes. The spark of life extinguished, just like that.'

'I know,' whispered Jenny. She swallowed with difficulty. 'My father died on Twelfth Night. One moment he was there, the next he was gone. You know at once, don't you? But I still didn't believe it. I'd got used to him being ill — and it had been a very long time since the doctor told us the illness was fatal. I was so shocked that it had actually happened. And then, when I realised, when the whole awfulness sank in, I was lost. I have never felt so alone.'

The children's untroubled breathing was the only sound in the room. As the candle flickered, Adam's hand found hers in a silent handclasp. No words of sympathy, nothing more intimate to shatter her control. Just simple fellow feeling. She squeezed his hand back in acknowledgement, trying to impart the same comfort to him.

'Go back to bed,' he said at last. 'The night is a dangerous time for confidences. We can talk, or not, as you wish tomorrow, when we have the bright light of day to remind us of obligations and promises.'

It was an odd thing to say. Jenny frowned over the phrase as she gave the straw in her pallet a couple of unobtrusive thumps. Adam had obligations for sure, with his children and the troupe. He couldn't know that she had them too.

★   ★   ★

Cousin Vincent had already interviewed Mr Tweedie, the steward, the gamekeeper and the butler. Finally it was Jenny's turn to be summoned to the study. She wept silently to see the changes the new Earl had already made to Papa's lovely room.

He didn't look up. 'For how much

40

longer do you and your companion intend living off my bounty? By my reckoning you have been a drain on the estate for some four months.'

Anger surged in Jenny, but she beat it down. 'I stayed to administer Rooke Hall, as I did for the last few years of my father's life. Board and lodging commonly form part of such a post.'

His cold grey eyes met hers. 'For a good male administrator, possibly. You are neither. The land here could be a great deal more productive, the rents are far too low, and the servants scandalously spoilt.'

With a strong effort, Jenny held on to her temper. 'I continued my father's policies and would do so again if the case arose. The solicitors were happy enough, knowing I was honour-bound to look after the estate and the people for whom we provide a livelihood.'

Her cousin gave an incredulous laugh. 'Our lands exist to serve us, not the other way around. As do those who live off our benevolence.'

41

'I am sorry you feel that way,' said Jenny in a low voice. Her heart bled for her home and their people. 'I will make arrangements for us to go by the end of the week.'

She could not live in the Prior's House yet, but Caroline Rothwell would take them in until the building work was finished. In a way, it would be a relief to leave. It was even more painful than she had expected to see another master here. After setting her packing in train, Jenny recollected that she had promised to read Eddie a story. Poor little boy, growing up in such a cheerless household.

The nurse, Ruth, heard of her departure with a nod. 'Thought it wouldn't be long. You're too friendly with us for one thing, and for another, no man wants a poor relation on the premises when he's looking out for a rich wife. Where will you go?'

A poor relation? Was that how they thought of her? Jenny was honestly amazed. She would have her own house and more than a competence when her majority was reached.

'We shall stay in Newmarket for the time being,' said Jenny. 'My friend Caroline is going away, but Aunt Sophy and I will be made very welcome in her house. It is less than four miles from here, so I can continue to visit Eddie.'

Ruth pursed her lips. 'I'd stay away once you're gone, if I were you, m'lady. At least you have the option.'

Jenny frowned. 'As do you, surely? Eddie would miss you, but if you are unhappy in my cousin's service, you have only to give notice and find a new position.'

'Bless you, we can't none of us do that. We're slaves.'

Jenny was so shocked she couldn't find words. 'That's impossible. Slave trading has been abolished these ten years!'

'Slave trading may have been. I never heard they outlawed slave owning. We belong to the Massa, body and soul.' Ruth eyed the pretty young African maid who was tidying the far end of the nursery. 'Some of us more than others.'

'Ruth, there is no slavery in England. You can leave in perfect safety.'

'So you say, m'lady. Myself, I like my skin right where it is.'

Jenny gathered Eddie on to her lap, profoundly alarmed. How could she convince Cousin Vincent's retinue that they were safe in England? Her mind whirling, she started to read aloud the legend of Demeter and Persephone.

The child listened, absorbed, his small body shivering. 'Mama is dead,' he piped up. 'Can I go into the ground to find her and bring her back?'

'No, it is only a story. Your mama is in heaven, as is mine, and my papa too.'

And she was alone with the weight of her people on her, and nothing she could do about it until she reached her twenty-fifth birthday and at last gained unrestricted access to the Prior's Ground and her mother's funds.

4

Jenny woke to Lottie's hand rocking her shoulder. Emerging from sleep, it seemed to her that every bone ached from contact with the ground. She reflected she had best become accustomed to this, and soon. She had not realised how soft and spoilt she was.

They were alone in the office. Adam and his son evidently started their day early. 'I've fetched the water for washing,' Lottie was saying. 'We always have to wash to be respectable.'

Jenny sat up, trying not to wince at the protest from her muscles. 'Also to be clean,' she murmured.

Lottie dismissed this adult whimsy, explaining that the company must placate the townsfolk by appearing respectable if they were to be allowed to act. 'But sometimes we have to move on even then.' Her indignation appeared to be more for the wasted ablutions than for the obtuseness of the neighbourhood.

'I daresay there are some companies who are not as well behaved as the Chartwell Players. Maybe those towns have been bothered by them. For my own part, I always look forward to a travelling theatre. One can always . . . ' Jenny stopped. She had been about to say '*take a footman if it looks rough*'. 'One can always find something to enjoy,' she said instead.

Breakfast was porridge from Mrs Jackson's large pot. Jenny decided for the sake of her digestion that it wasn't the same large pot that had held yesterday's broth. She ate hungrily, glad of the warmth. The weather this summer had not been kind, and today there was a dank chill to the early morning air.

'Sometimes,' whispered Lottie over her own bowlful, 'when we live in lodgings, we have eggs and ham. When we stayed at Kydd Court, which is

Susanna's big house, she had a cook and we ate and ate and ate. Will was so full he could hardly walk to the stables.' She giggled at the memory.

Will. That was Adam's son, whom Jenny had not yet met. She glanced around, but there were no boys to be seen amongst the company. 'Is Will with the horses now?'

Lottie nodded. 'Yes, but soon he must be back to rehearse his scene. He likes horses better than people, apart from me and Papa. He liked it *really* at Kydd Court. When we are in Newmarket, he goes to Penfold Lodge stables to learn from Mr Flood. That is Susanna's house as well, but Caroline lives there really.'

Jenny hoped the involuntary clatter of her spoon into her bowl at this artless confidence hadn't been remarked. Rooke Hall was not four miles from Newmarket, and she didn't want anyone in the company to connect her with the area. It would only take one loose word spread abroad to expose her if her cousin set investigations in motion. She saw Mrs Jackson looking across. 'Who are Susanna and Caroline?' she asked with what she hoped was the right degree of disinterest.

'Our friends. Susanna stopped being an actress when she married Mr Kydd, and now she has a baby. Mama is buried in the churchyard in their village.' Lottie bit her lip. 'We were very sad, but she is safe in heaven and doesn't hurt anymore. Will and I thought we might stay at Kydd Court and live in a real house all the time, but Papa said he finished with grandness a long time ago and we must carry on.'

'It's the players' way,' pronounced Mrs Jackson. 'A decent burial and on with the motley. Sentiment doesn't pay the bills.'

Jenny ducked her head. Mourning could indeed take place inside oneself just as well as with external show, but it was still a heartbreaking story.

After breakfast came the rehearsal. As much as Jenny would have liked to watch, she had been struck by an idea of enormous cunning. 'I must write a letter,' she said to Lottie. 'It will not take long, and if you are not needed at the rehearsal, you may come with me to post it.' She got out her writing case and, as she had hoped, Lottie immediately wanted to write a letter as well. But who to? She didn't know anyone.

Jenny made a show of thinking. 'You could write to Susanna, perhaps. You can send your love to the baby and the cook, and say your new friend Jenny Castle has given you a sheet of her nicest paper and has drawn a little bird in the top corner.' With a few strokes of her pencil, she did so.

'It's a wren,' cried Lottie, delighted. 'We see them in the hedges sometimes, but the eggs are too tiny to eat. Are you putting one on your letter as well?'

'Yes, I always do. It is a small joke, because Papa used to call me his little jenny wren. If I ever didn't draw one when I was away from home, he knew something was wrong and would write to send for me.'

As they wrote side by side, Jenny quickly, Lottie laboriously and with tongue sticking out, Lucy Jackson passed by on her way to the rehearsal. 'A quaint picture,' she said with a laugh. 'I congratulate you on beginning your duties so fast, but you will never get Will to settle to his letters like that.' Her eyes flicked over Jenny, evidently gratified to find her own person superior in every way.

'Lucy, we are waiting!' Adam's voice carried sharply from the stage.

Instantly Lucy's demeanour changed. 'Coming,' she trilled as she tripped away. 'Have I held you up? I was helping Lottie.'

The little girl's eyes met Jenny's. 'She is very pretty,' she said with eight-year-old candour, 'but she tells awful bounders.'

While they waited for the ink to dry, Jenny tied her one frivolous bonnet over her inexpertly pinned hair. Lottie ran to release her brother from the rehearsal so he could show them where the mail office was. Will proved to be about ten years old, Adam in miniature, big for his age and stocky, with a shock of straight dark blond hair and a suspicious scowl. 'I don't need teaching,' he announced by way of introduction.

Jenny opened her eyes wide. 'Goodness, no, I can see you are far too old for the schoolroom. But if you could give us your escort to the main part of the town, I would be most grateful.' She paused, her head to one side. 'I wonder if there is a baker or some such nearby. I have *such* a craving for a penny bun.'

Lottie beamed. 'There is, there is! Come on.'

'Wait — we must add the directions.' Jenny folded the letters and sealed them with a couple of wafers. She wrote the address on hers and just caught herself before writing Susanna's. The children were not supposed to know she was Susanna's friend. 'May we interrupt your father for Mrs Kydd's address?'

Lottie subsided. 'Papa hates disturbances. We'll have to wait.'

'I know the direction,' said Will gruffly.

Jenny printed as he dictated, reflecting that he sounded as if he had learned it by rote. She hoped he was less wooden playing parts on the stage.

'Who is yours to?' asked Lottie as she danced along, waving the letters to dry the ink.

'I will tell you if you walk beside me like a respectable young lady and not a performing monkey. We do not want to be the cause of having to leave this nice town, now do we?'

Lottie giggled and slowed to a demure walk. She peered at Jenny's handwriting. 'Mr Tweedie. Who is Mr Tweedie?'

'My late papa's man of business. I have told him I have found the Chartwell Players and am living with you. He might wonder where I was, else.'

Will shot her a shrewd look. 'Have you run away?'

Jenny experienced a slight shock. She hadn't expected someone so young to be so quick. Evidently he took after his father in more than appearance. 'In a manner of speaking, yes,' she said, choosing her words carefully. 'My family wanted me to do something that I had no wish to comply with, so I thought I would come and stay with you until they had forgotten about it.'

'Tweedie, Tweedie, Tweedie,' chanted Lottie softly. 'It's a funny name. What does he look like?'

Jenny smiled. 'He is a most respectable elderly gentleman with thin jerky legs and spectacles. When he is worried, he takes off his glasses and polishes the lenses all the time.'

Lottie laughed up at her, charmed. 'And is he polishing them now?'

'I think he might be,' said Jenny. 'That is why we must get my message to him as soon as we can, to set his mind at rest.'

After confiding the letters to the mail, and disposing of roughly double the quantity of penny buns that Jenny had budgeted for, she asked about the company's horses. Will became loquacious on the subject and was so well pleased with finding her not only interested, but also perfectly able to tell a hock from a harness, that the three of them repaired to the stable to meet the animals in person.

All in all, thought Jenny as they returned to the theatre, it had been a morning well spent. First and foremost, she had the children's confidence. This was most important. Children needed to know that there was someone who would always be on their side. Jenny was fond of youngsters. Motherless ones had an especially dear place in her heart. If she hadn't achieved this one thing, she would have felt bad indeed about using the Chartwell Players for cover. The side benefits for *her* were that anyone looking for a solitary grieving female would pass over a lady in a frivolous hat in company with a couple of affectionate children — and the longer she spent with them, the more the Chartwell Players as a group would associate her with the Prettyman family, should questions ever be asked.

* ★ ★

The rehearsal had finished by the time they got back. Members of the company were preparing to walk towards the town.

'That is a livelier bonnet than the one you were wearing last night,' said Adam. 'Pretty colours suit you.'

Behind his shoulder, Lucy Jackson did not look best pleased.

'Thank you,' said Jenny. 'I have been thinking I must get some ribbon to trim my old one. Perhaps Lottie and I will find a haberdashery tomorrow, if you do not require her.'

'There will be lots of stalls when we get to Midsummer Fair,' said Lottie. 'Lots and lots.'

'You'll need to take young Will with you to guard your purse when we get there,' warned Mrs Jackson. 'It's not a place to wander off without an escort. I certainly don't let my girls out of sight without they have a stout arm under their elbow.' She looked significantly at

Adam as she spoke. Lucy blushed prettily.

'It's crowded enough,' agreed Adam. 'Cambridge is good and central. That's why we go there, for the business. Plenty of customers with coin to spend and plenty of vendors with money in their pockets. All of them ready and willing to be entertained.' He glanced at Jenny's feet. 'You'd do better visiting the cobbler than the haberdasher. We've a way to travel. You'll be needing good soles to your boots.'

Lucy smirked. Adam ducked inside the theatre, leaving Will to return to the stables and the Jacksons to resume their walk into the town.

'Is it Midsummer Fair soon?' asked Jenny, following him through the doorway. Today's stroll with the children had been taxing enough. She'd hoped to recover from yesterday's journey from Newmarket before moving on anywhere, and Cambridge must be thirty miles from here.

'It's approaching.' He had his back to

her, staring at the stage. 'You were lucky to find us here. We play tonight, then we will pack up and be on our way.'

* * *

Adam kept his gaze fixed on the stage, aware of Jenny behind him, willing her to go through to the office and put her purchases away or take her bonnet off or any of the other small busy things women did when they were fashioning themselves a nest. The truth was, she unsettled him. She was from a different world. The way she'd gone outside last night without putting boots on first, for instance. It was a long time since he had been as green to the travelling life as she was. She brought back memories he thought he had suppressed.

After a moment, he caught the quiet sound of the passage door. He relaxed. This was his world now. This was his nest, his way of life. He moved around, straightening benches, picking up the odd scrap of debris. It was in a barn very like this that his passion for the theatre had ignited when he was younger even than Will was now. Back before he had any thought that the touring stage would one day become his life. The annual visit by Mr T's company to the neighbourhood, for which he had saved his pennies all year so he could watch night after night as long as the run lasted. He smiled to himself ruefully. The magic and awe of being inside a story as it unfolded in front of him had never worn off.

The children had copied the plays afterwards, of course, and acted out their favourite scenes amongst themselves, but for Adam it had been something more. He recalled the reluctant admiration from his older brothers when he mimicked the actors, word and gesture perfect. The heady realisation that here at last was something he could do better than them. The sheer chest-busting triumph of making people laugh. It was quite some narcotic.

Would his playing tonight inspire a child to take up acting? And if it did, would that be good or bad? He shook his head free of the fancy. As if it mattered anyway. Provided the Chartwell Players' capering amused the townsfolk for a space, they would welcome the company back. Adam asked very little more than that.

Behind the stage now, he heard Lottie chattering and Jenny's low murmured responses. Jenny. Now there was a puzzle he ought to make more of a push to unravel. It had been so strange to hear another adult breathing in the darkness with them last night. He wasn't quite sure how he'd allowed her to stay, and he still didn't know if the arrangement was advisable; but Lottie was already disposed to love their new guest, so for that alone he must make Jenny welcome. He did hope, though, that this wasn't Susanna's misguided attempt at matchmaking, or both she and Jenny would be disappointed. If he had learned nothing else these past months, it was that he had never been, and never would be, a fit husband for any woman.

Thinking of which, he berated himself for praising Jenny's bonnet when Lucy was within earshot. All he had meant by it was a simple compliment, because the pretty colours had lifted her gentle expression and made her look less watchful.

Now Lucy would overact off and on the stage, and he would again have his work cut out to convince her of his disinterest. Why were very young women so foolishly apt to fancy themselves in love on the flimsiest of pretexts? Lucy and Grace had both grown up in the company, for goodness sake. He put it down to Mrs Jackson. If girls' thoughts were given a proper direction by the adults around them, life would be far smoother. His own calf-love many years ago, for instance, would have subsided into a pleasant, melancholic adoration had it not received any encouragement. Then he would have been spared the devastating knock-back to his pride when he learned he was considered too poor a catch for anyone to consider seriously.

But then if that had not happened, neither would the consequent events, and he would not be here now. Without the false hope, he would have seen his first tentative sweetheart bestowed on a doting landowner old enough to be her father with nothing more than a healthy regret. He might even have danced at her wedding.

Ah well, it was an ill wind that never blew anyone any good. Chloe had given him the lyrical sensation of first love that he could now summon up when he played Romeo. His chest tightened at the inevitable following thought. She had also indirectly given him the blind rage which he tried *not* to overwhelm him when fighting Tybalt. Shakespeare had it right. Love makes of us all such fools.

5

That night, Jenny was to start on her bookkeeping duties by assisting Billy Bidens in the taking of the ticket money. Billy was a showily dressed, well set up fellow, the younger of two brothers who were attached to the company. Jenny could see why he was on the door, for he was a fast talker, ready with compliments for the ladies and jokes for the gentlemen to welcome them to the play; but he was certainly not as pleased at the addition of a female companion as his conversation would give one to expect. She sat at a small table, the better to organise the takings. Billy lounged against the door of the barn, laughing in a mocking, good-natured way with the customers when she wasn't as quick as him to tally the sums due. Jenny did not rise to the bait, noting that while his fingers were

62

as fast as his tongue, *hers* were a deal more accurate in the giving of change. It was astonishing how many times he mistakenly gave only five pennies in change when a shilling was tendered for a sixpenny seat. And that was only the ones where the customers noticed.

As the first song commenced, he made to sweep the loose coins together. 'I'll give the money to the governor to put in his strongbox.'

She smiled at him. 'There is no need. I am the bookkeeper now, so I will enter the figures into the ledger straight away. Pray do not let me keep you from your entrance.'

He seemed less pleased than ever as he walked away. Jenny looked thoughtfully after him. Was he wary of her because she was new? Or for another reason? Adding the money, her suspicions grew. She ran her fingers down the column. If Adam's scrawled figures were to be believed, the sum was up five full pounds on the previous evening.

'Billy Bidens robbing us?' Adam was

shocked when she spoke to him quietly at the end of the performance with a request that he lock the money away. 'No, I cannot believe it. You must be mistaken. Why would he do that?'

Could anyone be so naive? But Jenny saw that he had not yet wholly thrown off the part he had been playing on stage, so modified her response. 'For gain, Adam. Surely you must have remarked that the world is full of those who line their pockets at the expense of others.'

'Naturally, but I would as lief not think my company numbers them.'

An idealist. Heaven bless the man. 'I daresay the majority of your troupe is as honest as the day is long,' she replied. 'It would be astonishing, however, if you never picked up any bad apples along with the rest of the harvest.'

Adam took a distracted turn about the office. 'I cannot dismiss him without proof. And we will be down two actors, for his brother will go with him. Forgive me, Jenny, but you have only been here for a single perfor-mance. Is it possible the takings are up because it is our last night in Clare for a while?'

'Why yes, that could easily be the case. I have no knowledge of the pattern, and I do realise I am new to this. Even so, Billy *was* very careless when giving out the change. That cannot be advantageous when it comes to retaining the good will of the district. Might I suggest that I collect the money from now on, with one of the other men to stand guard and to check I am not robbing you in my turn?'

He scrubbed a hand through his hair. 'It seems a sensible measure. But if Billy *is* dishonest, I should not have him in the company.'

He looked so troubled that Jenny was moved to touch his arm. 'Not putting him in the way of temptation may be all that is necessary.'

He nodded. 'Aye, and be alert for the potential elsewhere.' He looked at her and she saw the way the fresh responsibility settled into his face. 'My thanks.'

He was a most disarming man, in general decisive, but reduced to helpless dismay when faced with money matters. Jenny concluded that it was indeed as Susanna had told her: his wife had used to deal with all their finances and had spared him the details of any problems. She thought back to those hurried plans, made last month in Caroline's private sitting room when it became clear Jenny would have to get away from her cousin. Susanna told them Mary had sublimated herself and her doings for her husband's art, even though he had never asked her to. What had her words been? '*You will certainly be welcome there, Jenny, for Adam must be desperate by now. Truly, I do not believe he was aware of half the business Mary took care of. She was so fierce, so determined that nothing should interfere with him being the greatest actor-manager who ever toured the country, that she did not allow any disruption to his work.'*

A laudable enough aim, thought Jenny, and perhaps Mary considered Adam had responsibility enough to deal with. But surely it was only by facing difficulties and overcoming them that one acquired the confidence to face them again? A plant confined in too small a pot, even when fed daily with the gardener's special nutrient liquid, might be a thing of beauty, but it would never fulfil its true potential.

She shivered, thinking of her cousin who *did* demand to know all that went on around him, and who furthermore required complete obedience from his household in the carrying out of his orders. It was not at all in the same case; but even so, she wished she had not brought him to mind quite so close to her night's sleep.

★ ★ ★

'So, you have seen fit to grace us with your presence at last.'

Jenny looked at the earl in surprise as she descended from her carriage, having just taken a large quantity of her belongings to store in Caroline Rothwell's attics. 'I beg your pardon, cousin. I was not told you wished to speak to me.' And she would not have guessed any such thing, considering he had been ignoring her as if she was so much empty space on every occasion this week when they had happened to be in the same room.

Cousin Vincent was simmering with anger, the very picture of a man ready to find fault with something. He appraised her equipage with hard eyes. 'The groom informs me this is your personal carriage. It was, however, undoubtedly bought with profits from the estate and therefore should be considered part of it. In future you will ask my permission to use it.'

He was intimidating, but Jenny was bolstered by knowing this section of the entail backwards. 'The carriage was bought some years ago by my father out of his legal income from the estate,' she said in an apologetic but firm voice. 'It was therefore his personal property and was given to me as a gift.'

The pale grey eyes were stony. 'As, so I discovered this morning, was the portion of this estate known as the Prior's Ground. The farms between Rooke Hall and the watercourse that I was under the impression belonged to me.'

Jenny was astonished. To hear him, you'd think he had been considering the Prior's Ground as his own for years. But as he had never been in touch with them apart from the brief notices of his marriage and Eddie's birth, he couldn't have known anything about the estate until his arrival in the country a few days ago.

'The Prior's Ground was purchased after the entail on the estate was set up,' she explained. 'My father settled it on my mother at the time of their marriage so she would always have an income of her own. On her death, it came to me. The Prior's House itself was habitable until the last century, and will be so again when the repairs I have set in motion are completed. My father has always kept the accounts strictly separate.'

'That anomaly was what drew my eye. You are fortunate to have the rents from the farms to draw on for expenses. They are the most profitable on the estate.'

There was a very hard edge to her cousin's voice. She knew from listening to his dinner conversations with the steward that he did not believe in women having independent means, though this had not prevented his demanding a list of all the eligible, rich, well-connected women in the area on his very first evening. Mr Tweedie had been most shocked.

'The two Priory farms are small and worked in the traditional manner,' said Jenny, carefully misunderstanding. 'I daresay with your modern methods, the production from the estate farms will soon be far superior.'

Cousin Vincent's hand clenched the handle of his whip. 'Not without access to the watercourse for increased irrigation,' he hissed.

Ah. Jenny now saw exactly why her cousin was so enraged and where the conversation was heading. A craven, peacemaking part of her advised granting him the right to cross her land without further ado, but she knew it would be a dangerous privilege. On very short acquaintance, her cousin had proved greedy, ruthless and ambitious. He would take and take — and ruin her farms as he did so. She stood frozen, unable to move, unable to think what to say. The whirr of the stable clock preparing to strike saved her. 'Excuse me, I must change for dinner if I am not to keep the household waiting.'

But Cousin Vincent was the one who did not appear for dinner. According to the grooms, he had left for London in a powerful hurry the instant she quit the stable block. He was almost certainly going to bother poor Mr Tweedie about the limits of the entail. An early retreat seemed advisable. Working through the night, she corded more trunks for Caroline's attics and packed the last of her day-to-day effects.

Visiting Eddie next day to say goodbye, Jenny found him listless and shivering and attended only by Bella, the young nursery maid. The young woman appeared far more interested in looking out of the window than in looking after her young charge. Her shrug bordered on insolence as she said Eddie often got like that, the same as his mama had done.

Jenny was torn. Surely she could spare half an hour to cheer the little boy up? She took him down to the kitchens and tempted him with a roll fresh from the oven and a glass of milk warm from the dairy. Then they went outside and played bat and ball for a little while. Jenny was gratified to see the colour coming back into his cheeks. She sighed as she hurried him back to the nursery. *She would miss him.*

The interlude had cost her valuable time. Cousin Vincent arrived back in a welter of flying hooves and swirling capes before she could leave, demanding hot food, wine, and all his household in attendance. Jenny thought it prudent to stay.

Dinner was fraught. Aunt Sophy chatted amiably as usual, but it was only the knowledge that she could do nothing if she was faint with hunger that kept Jenny eating. Swallowing food down was nearly impossible with Cousin Vincent staring assessingly at her and refilling his glass with increasing frequency throughout the meal.

'What will you do when you leave here?' he asked suddenly.

'Aunt Sophy and I will stay in Newmarket until the Prior's House is finished,' replied Jenny in a composed voice. Oh, how she wished the trustees had acceded to her request that they release part of Mama's inheritance early. She could have hurried the

73

renovations through by now. Unfortunately, until Papa had also actually passed away, they had been inflexibly obdurate on the matter.

Cousin Vincent's eyes narrowed at the mention of the Prior's House, but he said, 'It would surely be more convenient for you to remain here at Rooke Hall. You would then be within a brisk daily walk of the workmen. I have always found close personal supervision to be essential in these matters.'

Jenny's alarm intensified. This was the first time her cousin had ever shown any interest in her plans. She did not believe for one moment that he had become enamoured with her company overnight. This was to do with his visit to Mr Tweedie. Did he think to persuade her to sell the Prior's Ground to him? Or, God forbid, wed her to gain control of it for his heirs? The way he was looking at her made her skin crawl.

The silence stretched. His hand, she

noticed, was unnaturally still. A muscle jumped under the surface of the leathered skin. Fear tugged at her like a rabbit in a snare, and she had to resist the urge to leap to her feet and run. Think. She must pretend to fall in with his wishes until she understood his intentions, then slip away with Aunt Sophy once his suspicions were lulled. 'The idea has merit,' she said hesitantly.

Cousin Vincent's hand relaxed. He picked up his glass. 'In return for your accommodation and that of your companion, you will spend time tutoring my son. One other matter. I have invited a number of my business acquaintances to visit. All-male parties have nothing to do with nursery wings or single females.' He smiled thinly. 'I suggest you walk carefully.'

* * *

Jenny jerked awake, her brow beaded with sweat. That was how it had started.

She forced herself to breathe deeply, forced her terror to subside. She was sixteen miles away from Cousin Vincent, and tomorrow they would be moving further still. All she had to do was to stay hidden amongst the Chartwell Players for the next four months, and he would no longer have the power to disturb her dreams.

6

Adam walked alongside the foremost wagon as they plodded in the general direction of Cambridge, keeping an eye on the road for the deeper ruts. Rain dripped off the brim of his hat. He looked sideways at Jenny, cheerfully mantled in her cloak and telling Lottie the story of brave Odysseus, roaming the seas for ten long years and having adventure after adventure while his patient wife waited at home.

'I wouldn't wait at home,' declared Lottie. 'I'd fight the monsters too.'

'Then you'd be in the way,' said Will from the seat where he was driving the wagon. 'Men would get killed protecting you.'

'They would not! If Penelope had gone with Odysseus to look after him, he'd have come back sooner. Mama said a family always stays together.'

And look where it had got her, into her grave because she cared more for him than he cared for her. Adam cleared his throat and shook his head angrily, the lightness he'd been feeling whilst listening to Jenny's tale gone. He knew everyone blamed him for Mary's loss. They couldn't think worse of him than he thought himself.

★ ★ ★

All the time she was talking to the children, Jenny was aware of Adam walking beside her, withdrawn somewhere deep inside himself. When Lottie mentioned her mother, Adam shook his head angrily. Not cross with Lottie, Jenny deduced, but angry at himself.

'*It isn't Adam's fault that he's so driven,*' Susanna had said, just a hint of impatience in her voice. '*Leastwise, not all his fault. Mary had a very strong personality. In order to justify eloping, she had to believe with her whole being that Adam was the greatest actor who*

78

ever lived. She kept day-to-day irritants from him. It became a habit with her. She was proud of it. He didn't notice how far her illness had progressed because she didn't tell him. It was reprehensible of him, of course, and at first sight it is difficult to see how a loving husband could be so blind, but she made him blinkered. She made him selfish. It is a terrible thing to say of one who was good to me and whom I counted as a friend; but in a dreadful way, by forcing Adam to be an actor-manager and not helping him to develop as a person, she brought her own ill-health upon herself.'

Mary had loved Adam, but she had been wrong in her dealings with him. Surely a marriage should be a partnership in all respects? Jenny's own mother had never been strong, but it had helped Papa to know that he was providing the best he could for her in the way of warmth and comfort and a good doctor.

All this was running through Jenny's head as they walked along. She was conscious of the fact that her cloak was becoming heavier with the rain, and that one of her boots was rubbing, but primarily she was wondering how to help a man who had not realised that he too needed to heal.

Break him out. That was the obvious answer. She had broken out of her physical bounds. He needed to break out of his mental ones.

'Careful,' he warned, and she saw she had been about to step into a water-filled rut.

'Thank you.' She looked through the rain at the fields and sighed. They desperately needed some weeks of fine weather to swell the wheat, dry it off and then get the harvest in. She had thought last summer bad, but this one was bidding to overtake it. And then there would be no grain available for bread, and those folk who did not have landowners to protect and feed them would starve. What of Rooke? Would Cousin Vincent look after the estate people?

Adam had heard the sigh. 'Are you

having second thoughts about travelling with us?'

'No, not at all. I am reflecting on the weather and wondering how everyone will be fed this year with the crops thin as winter and rotting in the fields.'

'As best we can. The clever landowners will dig deeper ditches to drain off the surplus water, layer what stalks there are in the barns to dry before threshing — and make a very pretty profit, no doubt.'

Jenny turned towards him, amazed. That was sound sense. Very sound indeed. So sound that she wondered if she could get a message to her tenant farmers at the Prior's Ground. But Adam had simply said it as a by-the-by, as easily as he had solved this morning's loading of the wagons. How would a travelling player have that knowledge?

★ ★ ★

It was only seven miles from Clare to Haverhill, but the rain had increased to

81

such ferocity by the time they reached the first houses that the horses could barely see the road on which to set their next step. Surely, thought Jenny, they would make a stop here?

'It'll have to be the inn,' muttered Adam, and drew the company to a halt next to the Queen's Head. A short time later, the wagons had been pulled inside a barn and the horses were being rubbed down in the adjacent stable.

Adam returned from negotiating with the landlord. As Jenny watched, she saw his back straighten, saw him become the company manager. 'Usual terms. We can play here if we hire their stabling and rent their rooms.'

There was a ripple of dissatisfaction. 'Methodists and Quakers,' grumbled a couple of voices.

Mrs Jackson shrugged. 'No more than we expected, and it's warm and dry,' she pronounced. 'Shall I go with you to get the licence?'

'If you would. We certainly can't travel any further today, so had best turn it to what account we can. Folk here will likely welcome the distraction from their looms and shuttles. Give them an excuse not to work in the poor light.'

Jenny went with him to fetch their belongings from the wagon. 'Why is the company not pleased to be staying in the inn?' she asked in a low voice. After two nights on a lumpy pallet on the hard floor, she viewed the Queen's Head as little short of Elysium.

'They have to pay for it,' said Adam. 'Coin in the innkeeper's pocket rather than in their own. Sleeping in theatres and wagons is free.'

'Oh, of course.' Jenny felt stupid for not seeing it before. But were they all in such dire financial straits as Adam? She followed him up the staircase, pondering. The Jacksons' clothes did not speak poverty, and an inn was vastly more respectable than setting up cooking pots and the like in a farmer's field. Why would Mrs Jackson choose to camp rather than hire lodgings? It was a puzzle.

Adam opened a door and gestured for her to precede him. She stopped in surprise. There were two large beds, hanging space, a table, a washstand, fireside chairs . . .

'You and Lottie will have one of the beds, Will and I the other,' he said, misreading her expression as he deposited one corded trunk and prepared to go back for another.

'It's not that. Adam, this must be the best room in the inn. Can you afford it?'

His face twisted. 'Haverhill is a God-fearing town. We need the goodwill of the magistrates to play here. If the manager of the company does not take the choicest accommodation, word goes around and we are decried as just another band of vagabonds.'

'Goodness, the things you have to think about,' said Jenny. 'I had no notion. What a good thing I joined you, for I can easily pay my share, and that Shylock downstairs will never know.'

Adam opened his mouth, but she

continued without giving him a chance to utter. 'You will not argue, please, Adam, for it will only waste time which you ought to be spending in getting ready. Do you go straight away to the magistrate? Should we ask for hot water so you can wash?'

'The landlord has sent his boy to find when I might call. Until then, the men and I will turn that back room of his into a stage. Jenny, I cannot let you — '

'If I were sharing with one of the women, I would pay half, would I not? Now, which clothes will you wear for the magistrate? I will hang them up for you. Unless you have learnt a way of packing that precludes creases? If so, I dearly wish you will teach it to me.'

Adam was not distracted by her levity. 'You are here for the children and for the ledgers. You cannot valet me.'

'It is not valeting, it is self-interest,' she countered. 'If you do not make a good impression, we will be outside in that rain again. I do not know about you, but I have a mind to be dry tonight; and if we can do it without cost to ourselves, so much the better.'

For a moment she thought he would demur, but then he gave an exasperated sigh and gestured to his trunk. 'There is a fresh shirt in there. Do you always have a reasonable argument for the things you are going to do anyway?'

She smiled at him. 'I find it helps.'

She was relieved to see an answering half-smile tugging at his mouth. They made another trip with the rest of the heavy baggage, and then Jenny left him sorting out the public room while she retrieved Lottie from the fascination of the inn yard to help her with the smaller items. She paused in the doorway, watching Adam's muscles strain under his shirt as four of the men manoeuvred the hinged frame containing the backcloth into place.

'Ingenious,' she murmured, realising that the painted canvas served the dual purpose of setting the scene and hiding the actors and equipment not needed on the stage. Lottie shrugged when

Jenny admired the cleverness. She'd been familiar with the theatre furniture all her days. It was nothing new to her.

They moved aside as the men headed through the passage to unload a similar contraption for the curtain. Not so Lucy Jackson, who artlessly let a hatbox fall from her piled arms as Adam passed. He didn't remark it, however, and it was left to Billy Bidens to scoop up the errant item with a smile and offer to carry it to the Jackson girls' room. It was noticeable that Billy felt himself well able to pass Jenny without offering to help, even though she was carrying twice as much.

Not that this portage was a bad thing, she reflected, lowering her bundles onto the bed and flexing her arms. A few more weeks of walking and hauling in the open air, and Cousin Vincent would never recognise the bustling woman with a stevedore's build as his pale, restrained relative. It would be another layer to her disguise.

She set Lottie to unpacking and went

back for the last load, smiling to see Will in the stable, grooming the horses and exchanging amicable insults with the innkeeper's lad. Nothing wooden about him there.

In the barn, Samuel Obidah was looking out at the curtain of rain.

'Where will you sleep?' she asked, remembering with some concern his preference for the stars.

He smiled gently at her. 'In here. Adam fixed it. Night watchman, see?'

Of course Adam would have fixed it. It was a company-manager affair. Jenny was getting his measure. He would remember Samuel and forget that his own cuffs were frayed.

In the back room everything was taking shape, the men working as an easy team with Adam in command. Jenny felt a twisting stab of guilt for her own people, left to fend for themselves on the land she ought to be protecting. She took a deep breath. She had had this conversation with herself before. It must be this way, for if she did not live long enough to secure her inheritance, they would be in a far worse case for good, not just for this one summer.

Meanwhile, she had a job to do. She would shake out Adam's clothes for the meeting with the magistrate, and then perhaps there would be a chance to settle down with the ledgers to see where they first began to go wrong. Though she might just write a quick letter to Mr Tweedie regarding the digging of deeper drains first.

* * *

Adam took the stairs two at a time, fury simmering in him. It was bad enough that Jenny was paying for half the room when she was in a sense under his protection, but he really could not allow her latest deed. 'Jenny,' he said, entering the chamber, 'Will tells me you gave him a penny to take your letter to the post.'

She and Lottie were sitting by the fire, each engaged in a piece of sewing. She looked up with a smile. 'Yes, was it not good of him? I asked if he could find out where the mail office might be, and he straight away offered to take it for me to save me getting wet.'

'As he should! Jenny, you cannot tip my children.'

Her eyes widened. 'Now you are being absurd. If the note had been to a house in the town, the footman would have given him a penny. Where is the difference? Why should Will not buy himself a sweetmeat as a reward for getting so very wet for me?'

Adam ground his teeth. Put like that, the gift did indeed sound reasonable. He stalked over to the window in frustration. Lottie had set out his things, making the inn room look like countless others they had stayed in; but something was different, some new ambience. He swung around. 'You have ordered a fire in here!'

Jenny looked naively pleased. 'I did. I remembered what you said about one sick person holding back all the rest, and as Lottie was shivering with the wet, I thought it best to get her warm so as not to succumb to a cold.'

Adam took two strides back to crouch by his daughter. 'Lottie? Are you unwell, sweetheart?'

'I am lovely and dry now, Papa, and Jenny has wrapped me in her very nicest shawl, see? She made it herself, though it was fiddly, and now she is showing me how to mend my skirt where I caught my boot in the hem.'

He looked up into Jenny's calm eyes. 'That was well done. Thank you.' His gaze dropped to the sewing in her lap. 'That is my shirt,' he said flatly.

She seemed unshaken by the disapproval in his voice. 'Lottie will be a good needlewoman with practice, but edging cuffs requires a skill she does not yet have. She is watching me, though, and learning.'

'Jenny . . . '

'Adam, I am not accustomed to being idle. I do not have enough of my own clothes to occupy me, so it would be a kindness to allow me to still my restless hands with your mending.'

He wanted to shout that he was not kind, that he minded very much. It wasn't simply chagrin that she saw the lack in his wardrobe and had appropriated to herself its restoration. She unsettled him. She was doing things Mary used to do, but in a different way, with no-nonsense despatch and a disquieting air of comfort.

She laid her hand lightly over his. 'It is one shirt, Adam. And tomorrow, if we are still held here by the rain, I will teach Lottie how to darn hose. Better by far to be gainfully employed, rather than getting in everybody's way.'

She said it as if talking about herself, but he knew she meant Lottie as well. Yes, better for his all-too-friendly daughter to be up here sewing, rather than chattering to every scoundrel who came walking into the inn yard.

'As you say.' He was outfaced, unbalanced, and he did not quite see how she had done it. He forced himself to meet her eyes again. 'Thank you.'

★   ★   ★

Jenny was glad for everyone's sake that the play that night was successful. Wet and dark though the day was, word must have gone around the town very quickly that a company of comedians was at the Queen's Head. Adam had chosen an old favourite, *She Stoops to Conquer*, fronted by a popular song and with an afterpiece to follow. Jenny enjoyed the evening as much as the audience.

Next day, the company gathered in the back room to discuss whether to stay another day or press on towards Cambridge.

'It's raining less, but the roads will be deep mud for a while,' said one of the older men.

'But if we stay, they will become worse.'

'Is there more money to be made at Cambridge than here?' whispered Jenny to Samuel, who nodded.

Adam came in, holding a letter

between his fingers. 'I think we have little choice. Our fame goes before us, it seems. We have been invited to play a bespoke at Radleigh Manor tomorrow night.'

Radleigh Manor? Jenny beat down a flutter of alarm. In happier days, her father had used to dine once or twice a year with old Mr Stavely at Radleigh Manor. But Mr Stavely had died some time ago and Radleigh made over to a nephew. Cards of condolence had been exchanged, but the younger generation were not known to each other by sight.

'A bespoke? Well, that's different,' said Mrs Jackson. 'Another night here with a full house will do us no harm.'

'Money, food and an increased reputation whenever we play a bespoke performance,' murmured Samuel in Jenny's ear.

But Radleigh Manor! Jenny slipped away, perturbed, leaving the discussion of plays and routes to the senior members of the company. She had been settling into this itinerant life. The mention of a family from her normal sphere was disturbing. She needed a period of reflection to determine how to deal with it — and with any other instances of the same sort that might occur.

7

It was very odd indeed being an invisible member of the company at Radleigh Hall when Jenny was accustomed to visiting such houses as a guest. She had tried to remain behind, saying that as she did not perform, she would be there under false pretences; but Lottie cried out that she must go, for there would be supper and pastries and other treats. When she saw the other members of the company looking at her curiously — a free meal such as were commonly put on for players not being generally turned down — she said placidly that in that case, she hoped the owners of the house did not tally up the actors on stage and compare the number with those eating.

The danger, she had seen on working it through, lay not in the gentry recognising her, but the servants. They would not be expecting her, of course; but any retainer of ten years' standing might easily trace Jenny's mother's features on her face and recall it later on, if notice of her disappearance were raised in the district. Cousin Vincent must surely be making some sort of effort to find her.

She took care to bow her head slightly and always work at Adam's or Mrs Jackson's directions during the unpacking of the wagon and the setting up of the stage. It would make her the more unremarkable. It was strange, though, once again to be walking on Turkey carpet instead of drugget, to be surrounded by polished wood and gleaming porcelain instead of deal partitions and glazed earthenware. The rest of the company stared at the furnishings with fascination. Mr Stavely had inherited a fortune from his Nabob father as well as Radleigh Manor from his uncle, and it showed. Jenny was chiefly struck by wondering whether she appreciated the luxury more after her few days on the road, or less.

The play chosen was *He's Much To Blame*. Jenny had seen it before and was in expectation of an amusing evening listening from behind the backcloth. Adam straightened his clothes prior to going down across the stage and through the curtains to deliver the monologue. In the salon, they could hear the rustling and chatter of a roomful of wined and dined guests. One voice stood out suddenly from the rest.

'Indeed, I am looking forward to the entertainment very much, Mr Stavely. I have been a patron of the theatre in Kingston these many years. Are you comfortable, Miss Stavely? Pray remove to this chair. I believe your sister is in a draught, Stavely. You will have to send for your glazier. It would never do for so charming an English rose to catch a chill.'

Horror swept through Jenny. She felt the blood stutter in her veins and might easily have fainted had she not been distracted by the sight of Samuel Obidah's face suddenly turning grey and the African stumbling towards the door.

On the point of parting the curtains, Adam's eyes snapped across.

'I'll go after him,' said Jenny on a whispered breath.

She heard Adam say, 'Take his lines, Chas,' as she forced her legs to carry her down the passage towards the wonderful, blessed, outdoor world.

Samuel was doubled over beside one of the outbuildings, retching and clammy and in no state to go back inside. Jenny was sorry for him, but relieved beyond measure that she had an unexceptional reason not to return to the house. She helped him to the wagon to lie down, then crept back to whisper to Lottie that she would stay with Samuel until the play was finished in case he needed her aid.

Lottie's eyes were fearful. 'It's not a fever? Not like Mama?'

'I do not believe so. It looks to me as

if poor Mr Obidah has eaten something that disagreed with him.'

'I will put some of the supper in a basket for him. And for you too.'

'Thank you, darling. That would be lovely.' But as Jenny slipped back outside, taking a wide berth past the kitchen regions where the visiting footmen and coachmen would be regaling themselves with bread and ale, she did not believe she would be in any better case than Samuel to appreciate Lottie's delicacies.

Her mind was all confusion as she struggled to absorb this new circumstance. She knew her cousin Vincent was ambitious, but how in the name of all unlikely occurrences did he come to be dining with Mr Stavely, and paying court to his very well-endowed sister by the sound of the exchange, after so short a time in this country? She hoped Miss Stavely had the strength to resist him. Or perhaps he might consider her rich enough to command some measure of respect once she was his countess. From what Jenny had experienced of the earl, it seemed improbable. She leant against the side of the wagon and closed her eyes.

★ ★ ★

'This soup is cold.'

The words dropped like rocks into the tension at the dinner table. Time slowed to a heartbeat as Jenny saw Cousin Vincent toss his spoon aside, move his hand to his hip, and send his whip snaking out to wrap three times around the server's forearm. The footman stood still, trembling, tureen and ladle in his hands.

'What did I say yesterday?' enquired Cousin Vincent.

The footman swallowed. 'As how it wouldn't happen again, my lord.'

'And yet it has.' He gave a sharp twitch to the whip, causing the tureen to upend down the unfortunate man's livery and fall heavily on his foot. 'Get that cleared up. Now.'

Jenny cleared her throat. 'This is the furthest room from the kitchen, cousin. Some loss of heat is to be expected.'

He didn't look at her. 'When I specify hot food I expect to be served hot food.'

The steward hurried into speech. 'If your lordship would consent to use the family dining room instead of this one, I believe your requirements might be more easily — '

'I am the earl! I will dine as befits my station! When I give a banquet, are my guests to eat cold collations? I think not.' His chilling gaze swept the room. 'It is very simple. If the members of my household cannot supply the basic necessities of life, I will replace them with those who can.'

★   ★   ★

Adam smiled and bowed and exhorted the company to do likewise. The ladies and gentlemen of the audience stood up and began moving out of the room.

Mr Stavely, by whose invitation the Chartwell Players were there, came across to Adam.

'Very enjoyable. Very enjoyable indeed. Cakes and such will be brought in to you presently. You'll see my steward for the fee.'

'Very generous of you, sir. I am glad we afforded you and your guests pleasure.' Adam had perfected his genial courtier act years ago.

'I did not see your African player tonight.' Mr Stavely's voice held the tiniest touch of petulance.

Adam controlled his pulse of anger. Samuel Obidah was an actor, not a curiosity to be shown off. 'I regret there was not a part for him in the pieces we performed this evening.'

'I'm surprised there are parts in any of your plays for a black,' said Mr Stavely's companion, a tall tanned man with cold grey eyes whom Adam disliked on sight. 'Do you have to beat his lines into him every night?'

Both men laughed, as if he had said

something amusing. 'The Earl of Harwood has recently arrived from Jamaica,' explained Mr Stavely in a careless tone. 'He has considerable experience in managing African workers.'

And Adam had considerable experience in keeping his tongue between his teeth. He deployed it now, smiling again and bowing. 'If you will excuse me, gentlemen, I must help my company clear your salon of our accoutrements.'

They moved away. Adam filled his lungs with air and expelled it slowly. Increasingly these days, he wondered whether losing himself in his acting on stage was sufficient compensation for tolerating some of his more pretentious patrons.

Lottie skipped up to him. 'Supper is ready, Papa. I said I would pack some for Jenny and Samuel in my basket. Do you think anyone will notice?'

Adam touched his daughter's cheek. 'And why would they mind if they do? You deserve extra, for you remembered all your lines today and charmed the ladies with your dance.'

'I know.' She tugged him towards the anteroom, where a large table had been set with food.

Mrs Jackson looked across and nudged Lucy, who delicately indicated the empty seat next to her. Adam felt another measure of impatience and instead followed Lottie around to where Will was already making inroads on the food. It *had* been a good performance tonight, but was it really enough, as he had always thought? Was he doing the right thing by his children, moving from place to place, chasing pennies? Did he want his daughter growing up like Lucy Jackson, perpetually on the catch for an actor one step up from her father? With Mary at his side, it had never seemed as if there was a need to follow any other way of life. Her vision for them had been unshaken, in sickness and in health. Since her death, though, he had had to step outside the confines of his role. He had discovered there were shoals to navigate that he'd been unaware of, and that he was unfit for as things stood. He had found there was, unexpectedly, still room for him to develop as a man. It was painful, but strangely exhilarating, or at least it would be once the money was straight. And it made him think.

★   ★   ★

Jenny woke when the company returned to the wagon. She was stiff and cold, and for a moment she knew a terrifying blackness until memory surfaced.

It was all right. She was safe and undiscovered. She must concentrate on the Chartwell Players rather than Cousin Vincent. There had always been the possibility that she might hear of him, since she had chosen to stay in the area rather than hide on one of her friends' estates for the next four months (and potentially have them accused of kidnapping her). It was encountering the earl so unexpectedly that had discomposed her. She moved across to Samuel, lying motionless in the corner.

'The performance must be finished. They are coming back with the crates. Are you feeling any easier?'

He uncurled. 'Yes,' he said on a soft sigh. In the light of the approaching flares, he didn't look as if he'd slept at all. 'I'll be better still when we're on our way.'

Jenny was at one with him there.

After loading the wagon, they started back to the village, where they'd taken lodgings for the night. Adam swung the lantern at one side of the road, and Mr Jackson held his on the other so Will could see where to guide the horses. The rest of the company followed or walked alongside. Jenny and Lottie joined Adam.

'It was good of you to stop with Samuel,' he said.

Guilt assailed her for the deception. She should tell him the truth. However, Lottie was within hearing distance so she put the disclosure aside for a better time. 'It was nothing. I was concerned for him, and as I was not needed inside, thought I might as well stay near.'

'You must have been cold.'

'My cloak kept me warm. It is thick and serviceable, even if it might not be in the newest mode.' She looked at his face in the shifting shadows, trying to lighten his expression. He was not usually this serious after a performance. 'Mama, you see, always believed in getting value for money, so it is as well I like it, for I daresay it will never wear out.'

She thought there was a brief smile, but couldn't be sure. Then Lottie stumbled, and Adam hoisted her up to share the wagon seat with Will. 'You are light,' he said when his daughter would have wriggled down. 'You'll not slow the horses, and we haven't so very far to go tomorrow.'

Jenny breathed in the night air and the scent of warm horse. This continual walking from place to place was not what she had envisaged, being far from her romantic imaginings of a strolling player's life, but it had a certain hard beauty to it. You pleased the people, the people paid. You enriched their lives and they made it possible for you to continue. But forever?

'Why do you do this?' she asked aloud.

Adam shrugged, not breaking his easy stride. 'Because I can.'

In another man she might have thought the answer flippant, but Adam had said it as the exact truth. 'Why not stay in one place, then?' she continued. 'Join a fixed company?'

'We had little choice. Mary was an excellent actress, but her powers of projection were poor. She could fill a booth or a barn or a drawing room with her voice, no more. As for me — look at the size of me. How could a regular company give me secondary parts when I'm bigger than their leading actors? I did not become an actor for a lifetime of playing third murderers or bumbling yokels.'

Jenny nodded, understanding the reasoning. 'Yes, I see. But why do you only stay for a night or two as we did at Haverhill, or a fortnight at most? The North and South Company of Comedians remain in a place above two months, I am sure.'

Adam gave a humourless smile. 'The Fishers have a large complement of players and they stay sixty days exactly, for that is the limit of the Act. Not me. I would not beggar folk who look to me to provide entertainment, who would pay out more sixpences than they can well spare, simply for light and warmth and to see us caper night after night.'

The lantern light caught his face from below, giving him an archaic cast. A strange feeling gathered in Jenny's breast and rippled through her body as she looked at him. What a sentiment; yet he had said it as a commonplace. This man was magnificent and moral. He would impoverish himself for people who never gave him a second thought once the evening's entertainment was over.

He cared. He cared about mankind

as a whole. Jenny already esteemed Adam Prettyman for his leadership of the troupe, but now she realised she admired him more than any other man of her acquaintance. Papa would have liked him too. No matter that their professions were different, for their codes, their inner cores were similar. For a moment, grief threatened to overwhelm her that the two men would never meet, but she beat it away, reflecting instead that with principles like those entrenched in his head, she had best sort out Adam's finances before he starved.

8

Cambridge. The Midsummer Fair. It was helpful, thought Jenny in retrospect, that she was wearing her plainest gown for their first full day here. Not that she had anything particularly modish with her, there being a limit to what could be packed into two valises that would have to be carried by hand; but it was insidiously comforting to know that she was in a decent high-necked cream cambric with a small fawn spot when there was a portentous bustle behind her in the supposedly private office.

'So!' said a voice quivering with outrage. 'As I thought! Loose women!'

Jenny looked up, alarmed, from the desk where she was at last beginning to make sense of the ledger. She saw a small round man wearing a costly coat, an elaborate watch-and-chain, and who was much puffed up with a sense of his own importance.

'I assure you, sir, I am not in the least loose,' she said, more acerbically than she would normally have addressed a stranger because of the fright he had given her. 'How dare you burst in on me like this? Is it possible that you have mistaken your direction?'

He inflated even more. 'My information is that there are immoral goings on in this booth.'

'Then your information is wrong. This is a respectable company of actors. I should not be here else. Furthermore, this is a private area, so I would ask you to please leave.'

He ignored her last sentence. 'And you are?'

She raised her eyebrows to underline his lack of manners. 'My name is Miss Castle. I am the bookkeeper to the Chartwell Players and governess to the manager's children. Sadly, there is no one here to introduce us. Whom do I have the honour of addressing? By what office do you invade my privacy without a by-your-leave or any attempt at advertising your presence first?'

'My name need not concern you.'

'Oh, but it does. How else am I to know who to complain of to the town authorities?'

'I, madam, am a concerned citizen.'

Jenny swallowed her rage. Adam would not thank her if she drove off all his potential custom. She must plough a different furrow here. 'And rightly so,' she said instead. 'One cannot be too careful if one is thinking of bringing one's wife to partake of an afternoon's entertainment. Now then, what is her partiality? A Shakespearian tragedy? After a display of traditional country dances, we play *Othello* today, which I think you will agree is a searing indictment of all those who allow themselves to be blinded by prejudice. If you prefer a contemporary piece, wait until tomorrow when you can watch *Wives as they Were and Maids as they Are*, written by Mrs Inchbald, who was, of course, born and bred not thirty miles away from here. I daresay you will not care for the melodrama which we put on by way of an afterpiece; but our Mr Farnell, who had a season at Covent Garden, will be singing some fine patriotic songs as the main entertainment of the evening.'

The man seemed to struggle for words. 'Don't think you've heard the last of this,' he said eventually. 'You ought to be ashamed of yourself.' Then he turned on his heel and left.

'That was very good,' said Adam, quietly from the dividing curtain between dressing rooms and office. 'Are you sure you aren't an actress?'

The encounter had left Jenny as taut as a strung bow. 'You know very well I am not,' she snapped. 'Tell me, does that happen frequently?'

Adam shrugged. 'Complaints? Oh yes.'

'Not the complaint. People coming into the tent like that from outside. I could have been doing *anything*.' More to the point, he could have *been* anyone. She had not yet forgotten the shock of nearly coming face to face with Cousin Vincent at Radleigh Hall. Suppose that had been him just now? Jenny gripped her pencil so hard at the terrifying thought that she lost all feeling in her fingers.

'There is little privacy on the road, especially in a fairground tent.'

'Well, there should be. How are you to earn respect if you do not enforce it?'

'Respect for a group of actors?' His voice was bitter. 'We are respected as long as we perform. No more.'

Jenny wanted to box his ears for accepting the situation this tamely. Why, when he was so alert to the needs of the rest of the world, did he never stand up for himself? It was enough to make her . . . No, she was in danger of being deflected here. She added Adam's baffling lack of self-esteem to the list of things she must deal with when the time was right and returned to the most important aspect of the morning's intrusion. 'Truly, Adam, I know we are all sleeping on the premises which will discourage prowlers at night, but is there no way to make this tent more secure during the day?'

'The fair employs constables to keep a watch out for thieves. Are you worried about the drinking booths robbing revellers of their discretion? We do not generally have problems.'

'But anyone can simply walk in at any time! If you are not worried for yourself or your strongbox, you should certainly be concerned for Lottie.'

Adam looked at her in resigned irritation, then gave a long sigh. 'I will see what I can contrive.'

★ ★ ★

To begin with, as he set up a trestle table across the door opening and drove extra pegs around the tent to lessen the gaps, Adam tried to work out why he was going to all this trouble. They had played fairs before with no ill outcome.

His steady rhythm with the mallet faltered as he remembered Mary's pleasure in being able to stock up on material and medicines and the small bits and pieces that made a travelling life comfortable. But he also remembered he and Mary had generally stayed in lodgings with the children for the duration of the fair, leaving the men to guard the tent and the company effects.

It was, he conceded as he put the tools away, possible that Jenny had a valid point. He routinely made sure the stage area was safe and that all the physical requirements of playing and getting the audience in and out were met. Now he looked around the large tent with different eyes. A dividing flap of canvas between dressing room and backstage was caught by a draught and buffeted him on the shoulder. Adam steadied it with his hand and stood there, considering. Yes, Jenny was right. The whole company was his demesne, and he should take care of more than just his craft. This curtain, for instance, and the others leading to the office and the main entrance. It would be a simple task to fix eyelets and lace the curtains in place when instant egress wasn't needed. He'd do it now. As he worked, he was surprised to find he was looking forward to the twinkling approval in Jenny's eyes.

⋆ ⋆ ⋆

Jenny stared upwards at the square of pale canvas that formed the roof. It had been a busy day, but she was finding it difficult to sleep. More stalls had been arriving by the hour, and now the night outside the tent was sprinkled with voices, loud and drunk, querulous and uncertain. Just two minutes ago, a couple of men with slurred voices had stumbled past, arguing about debts and cursed cards and ill luck. The Chartwell Players were to be here two weeks? It was likely to be the most unrestful fortnight Jenny had ever spent. She turned over, willing herself to relax. She had seen for herself that the tent was more secure and had thanked Adam. He'd brushed the praise off, but she thought he'd been pleased to have his work appreciated.

Relax, Jenny. Sleep. On the other side of the office, Adam's quiet breathing ought to reassure her, but she was jumpy. It might be that she was simply unused to crowds and the presence of so many people who might yet be a danger to her. She couldn't forget the officious busybody who had burst in on her this morning. As she drifted into an uneasy doze, a sudden shout close by brought memories swarming into her defenceless mind.

★   ★   ★

A horse's agonised scream, followed by a shot. The hoop that Jenny was teaching Eddie to bowl veered sideways and fell to the ground with a clatter. Eddie began to shake violently. Shortly afterwards, a groom's hack came galloping past towards the stables, foam dripping from its jaws and Cousin Vincent on its back. And a few minutes later came one of the grooms on foot, hurrying up the drive.

'He shot it,' he said to Jenny in disbelief. 'He shot his own horse! It shied at a rabbit, he struck out with his whip, it reared and unseated him. And he shot it. Clear through the brain.' The groom's throat worked as if trying to get a foul taste out of his mouth. 'I've been here man and boy, Miss Jenny, but I'll not stay further nor wait for my wages neither. Take the young master inside, lass. I've to check on my own poor beast and then get the carcase away.'

Jenny stared after him. She would indeed take Eddie indoors. Then she would direct the groom to walk her carriage pair and her riding horse over to one of her farms with coin for their livery and another purse for his own board and lodging. If Cousin Vincent noticed the absence, she would say she *was sparing the estate their daily expense. This afternoon, she would walk the couple of miles to the Prior's House to again impress upon the workmen the need for it to be habitable as soon as they could make it so. She could not live within the earl's orbit for much longer.*

As a shivering Eddie tugged her indoors, the horse's scream echoed in her ears.

★   ★   ★

A soft voice called her name. Jenny's eyes flew open. Thank God. She was in Adam's tent. She was safe. Cousin Vincent and his pistol and his ready whip were but a memory. She was hidden with the Chartwell Players. Aunt Sophy and their two maids were secure at Penfold Lodge with her groom and her carriage horses. Her riding horse was at the Starlings' farm. Thank God.

Grey dawn stippled the tent. She lay for a moment, letting the sweat on her body dry and her heart rate return to normal. Then she turned her head to see Adam, awake in his own pallet on the other side of the small office, propped up on one elbow looking at her. There was a concerned furrow on his brow.

'Are you distressed?' he said quietly. 'You were whimpering in your sleep.'

Whimpering? It was amazing that she had not yelled aloud with horror. 'I . . . I had a bad dream.'

'Several bad dreams, I think. I spoke your name and was debating whether to rouse you properly, but thought you might cry out louder.'

'Thank you. I wish you had done so. I had no desire to relive those particular memories, I assure you.'

He gave a half-smile. 'Then I shall wake you if the same thing occurs again. It was strange, for you are in general such a practical, composed person that it did not seem as if it *could* have been you making such a desperately sad sound. Would it help to talk about whatever is troubling you?'

Jenny hesitated. Her dreams had brought back the full horror and fear of those last days at Rooke Hall, and in truth she wished for nothing more than to lay her burden on someone else's comfortingly broad shoulders. But Adam had problems of his own. It would hardly be fair. There was little he could do, bar provide her with a refuge, and he was doing that already.

Then the moment was lost as Will stretched and yawned and wriggled himself free of his bedroll, asking with the hopefulness of the young whether anything was wanted from the cook-stalls.

All the same, Adam's gaze lingered on her in a worried fashion, and Jenny resolved that if he asked again, she would tell him the whole story.

★ ★ ★

Not well done, thought Adam, disgusted with himself. He should have pressed Jenny to tell him what was

124

amiss, instead of using Will's waking as an excuse to quit the tent. He sluiced his upper body down rather more vigorously than was necessary with water dipped from the Cam and instructed Will to do the same. This was his blindness with Mary all over again. Why must he always take the easy option? Forever shying away from difficult tasks just as the schoolmaster had sneered at him for doing years ago.

'It's all for nothing,' complained his son with some bitterness.

Adam was startled by the apt comment. 'Why do you say that?'

'Because it is.' Will eyed the pail as if he'd like to throw the water over his father for a change, rather than the other way around. 'I'll just get dirty again seeing to the horses.'

Oh, he was complaining about washing. For a moment, Adam had had the uncomfortable notion that Will could read his mind. 'Then you can clean up again afterwards,' he retorted. 'I'm not having customers thinking the

Chartwell Players are a bunch of rogues. One of the cits marched in on Jenny yesterday, denouncing our tent as a hall of shame.'

'I know. She was mad as fire. She's told Lottie never to go running off without her or one of us nearby. Didn't want some do-gooder picking her up and taking her to a house of correction.'

Adam felt a smile curl his lips. 'Did she say that?'

Will laughed. 'Yes, and then she got out that puzzle where you put the countries of Europe together, so Lottie could prove to everyone that she wasn't a ragamuffin.' He paused. 'It's a good puzzle. Lottie was quicker than me, then I learnt it and now I'm quicker than her. Some of the names are in the plays we do. It was funny, seeing them as real. Can we have breakfast now?'

They walked back and saw Jenny and Lottie coming to meet them with tidy clothes and braided hair.

'Look at you both,' said Jenny with a smile. 'A shining face and a shining heart, as my nanny used to say. Just let anybody try to tell me today that we are not respectable.'

A shining face and a shining heart. The words swam back from the past. It seemed Jenny was determined to undermine his barriers, one by one.

9

Wages day. Jenny had Mary's records
and knew there was enough in Adam's
strongbox to cover the weekly salaries.
What she was more troubled about was
the scribbled list of 'arrears' written in
the most haphazard fashion she had
ever encountered on one side of the
ledger. It seemed to cover the last few
weeks, but whether it was per week or
cumulative it was impossible to tell. She
would have to pin Adam down after the
morning rehearsal and ask him about it.
Accordingly, she separated him from
the rest of the company with a trifling
query and then drew him into the
office. Billy Bidens watched her inso-
lently and nudged his brother. Their
guffaws vexed her, but she was more
concerned with getting to the root of
the ledger's conundrums, and saving
Adam's face while she did so, than with

correcting any false impressions of her own forwardness.

'It is what we always do,' said Adam when she raised the subject of the arrears. 'If there is not enough money in hand, then some is taken off all the salaries and made up when we have a surplus.'

'Are each of these separate amounts that are owed, then?'

Adam looked cautiously at the ledger. 'Some figures might be added to the previous week,' he hazarded.

Jenny sighed. Perhaps she could ask Mrs Jackson. She'd bet her last shilling that the matriarch of the company knew exactly who was owed what. 'I had best work the columns from the other side and see what has gone out and what should have gone out.'

'Can you do that?' There was an air of awe in his voice. 'How do you come to be so proficient?'

She smiled faintly. 'I have been looking after my father's affairs for five years or more.'

'I remember you said he had been ill for a long time. Do you miss him?'

Her heart twisted. 'Every day. Which is why I must remain busy. When he died, I was as much distraught because I could not *think* as because I was grieving. I spent three days dusting all the books in the library until I could reflect logically again. My friends did not know what to make of me at all.'

He gave a small laugh, then said, 'Working with numbers is a skill I do not possess, as I think must be self-evident. I have often wished it otherwise, never more so than recently.'

Something in his tone made her glance up. 'No one can do everything. You have other skills more valuable for your daily life. I could never assemble this tent by eye, for example. I could not pack all those disparate pieces of curtain and staging into wagons the way you do.'

He looked surprised. 'But that is easy. There is always a best way for something to lie, or for two pieces to fit together.'

'Different skills,' laughed Jenny. 'It is as well we are not all alike.' She traced backwards through the ledger until she reached Mary's neat hand. 'Now then, this was January . . . ' and stopped, because Adam had ceased to pay attention. His eyes were on Mary's writing and his face was eloquent with despair.

Jenny felt a pang. How much he had loved his wife. And because she had always found it salutary to bury her own grief in work, she abruptly decided not to ask Mrs Jackson for figures, but to make Adam remember the details for himself. 'To start with,' she said aloud, 'when was the last time there was enough in the coffer to pay everyone's wages? I do not include yours in that, for it is plain you have been stinting yourself for months.'

★ ★ ★

Adam continued to gaze at the figures, his vision blurring. Stinting himself — ?

131

Jenny didn't know the half of it. As soon as Mary had first weakened, he had needed to dip into their savings for expenses. There was precious little left now. He wrenched his eyes away from the page. Even seeing her writing reminded him of his failure.

'January,' he said, hearing his voice drag. 'Susanna came to watch us play and saw immediately what I had not, that Mary was not merely sick, but dangerously ill. She and Kit swept us all off to Kydd Court and we set up in a barn there for six weeks. Mary, the children and I were in the house with them, and there were empty estate cottages for the company to stay in. I think it was the first time I have ever seen Mrs Jackson at a loss for words, at the circumstance of her family having a whole cottage just for them. The end of February was the last time the books were straight.'

And it was also the last time he had been at peace with himself. How could he have missed what was so glaringly obvious? How could he have been so appallingly blind? He stared back into the past, ambushed again by the horror of the moment when he realised how truly flawed he was.

Jenny's hand settling on his for a brief moment twitched him out of the familiar spiral of guilt. 'That was good of Susanna,' she said softly.

'She said it was what any friend would do. It comforted Mary to think that she would go to her final rest in a fixed, God-fearing place.' He gazed at the ledger, giving voice to his most private trouble, something he had never believed he could tell anybody. 'But it was *she* who had always insisted on the travelling life for us. Always. Was that just for me?'

How could he live up to the sacrifice of her life if so? How could he betray Mary by even contemplating giving up this strolling-player existence?

He could feel Jenny's silent sympathy. He didn't deserve it. He sighed. 'I left Kydd Court too soon after her death. Like you, I needed to be busy.'

'Lottie told me she thought about living in the kitchen there forever and getting fat.'

Adam smiled. 'Her and Will both, but I wouldn't impose. No, that's not why I packed us off on to the road again. There were too many memories there. One night Mary cried out, '*But what about him? Who will see to him?*' and wouldn't settle until she had been given more of the laudanum.' He glanced at Jenny's compassionate face. 'She had lost a baby some months before. Perhaps in her delirium she thought it still lived. Looking back, I realise losing the child was what started her decline. Shame on me for not seeing it at the time.'

Jenny gave his hand an admonitory shake. 'Hush. What good does it do to dwell on the past? You cannot change anything. She and the babe are reunited now, that's for certain. And *we* must get on with these accounts.'

Still in the grip of remorse, Adam felt

a degree of resentment at this intrusion of the mundane. 'You told me *you* could sort them out.'

'And so I will. But you must see that in order to pay your people what is owed to them, we must first be sure how much *is* owed. Now, what had you been playing the first time you noticed a loss?'

What had they been . . . ? But Adam found that he did remember very well, for his heart had been sick and full of shame, and he had chosen *Othello* in order to rant on stage. The audience in Northampton had been stunned, he recalled, and had flocked back the next night, which made it all the more surprising that there had not been quite enough in the bag at the end of the week.

By the end of two hours, Adam's opinion of Jenny had risen very high indeed. By patient (he wryly admitted it) questioning and encouragement, he had remembered every one of the weeks that he had thought lost in a blur of misery and self-reproach. He had recalled where the Chartwell Players had been and for how long, what they had played, who had been light with sums. He felt quite astonishingly empowered in regaining those months.

He smiled at Jenny's own unfeigned air of satisfaction as she finished her neat columns of figures. 'How did you do that?' he asked.

'With the application of logic. It is not a very womanly attribute, but it makes dealing with accounts considerably easier.'

He hugged her shoulders impulsively. 'Thank you. For more than just the accounts.'

She made a diffident movement under his arm. 'I do not believe,' she said, 'that it is always best for us to suppress memories which make us sad. It may be easier for a space, but I think we need them in order to be whole.'

Adam blinked. This was an alarmingly radical idea for one who had been burying smarts and lacerations deep inside him for as long as he could remember. Did she apply the principle to herself as well? He was about to ask what it was that troubled her sleep so often, but she became businesslike again.

'I have kept you from company affairs, but it was time well spent, don't you think?' she said. 'I feel a great deal more confident about turning the funds right side up again in not too short a time.'

He still had his arm around her, he realised. He withdrew it, not rebuffed, but reminded in the most natural, unembarrassed manner that theirs was a working arrangement. 'That would be a miracle that I am not sure I deserve,' he said, standing and stretching after so long hunkered over the books.

'Nonsense,' she said, smiling comfortably up at him. 'It is not for us to decide whether we are worthy. Miracles are given freely, else they would not *be* miracles, now would they?'

* ★ * ★ * ★

He had hugged her. He had hugged her
and for a moment his blanket of grey
had turned golden, as it was supposed
to be. Jenny had very nearly forgotten
to breathe in the wonder of it, so
pleased to have shifted his misery, so
proud to have let in a chink of light. His
arm was around her, casual like kin,
close like a lover, but he was lost in the
glorious sense of self-gain and this,
right now, was about his rehabilitation.
So she *had* breathed, and made some
workaday comment, and his arm had
slipped away quite naturally and he had
stood and stretched. There was the
tiniest sliver of time when Jenny was
not disappointed, not in the slightest.
All was as it should be. All was normal.

They dispensed the salaries together,
Jenny and Adam. Jenny was interested
to see that when she murmured to Mrs
Jackson how much she was still owed
from previous weeks, the older woman
nodded in agreement. She was also

interested to note that it was as Lucy had said — Mrs Jackson really did take charge of both her daughters' money.

All went well until it was the turn of Billy Bidens. He glanced at the coins in his hand then said with a disarming smile that he was afraid he had been short-changed.

Jenny was horrified when Adam's hand moved involuntarily to the money bag to fetch out an extra shilling. She knew Billy was lying. If he got away with it this first time, it would undermine her authority with the rest of the company. 'Are you quite sure?' she asked in a clear voice. 'Adam and I counted the wages most carefully. Everyone else has the right money. Perhaps you should check yours again.'

'See for yourself,' he said, slapping his handful down on to the table. He stood back in an attitude of gloating righteousness, but Jenny had heard the tiny chink of coins as he hooked his thumb into his waistcoat pocket.

'Very strange,' she said, 'I suppose

the missing shilling did not become lodged in your cuff when you scooped your pile off the table? I have often seen it happen with elaborate clothing such as yours.'

Just for a moment there was pure hatred in the man's eyes. 'Oh, keep your damn shilling,' he said as he swept the coins back up again and stalked away.

For one, maybe two seconds, nobody moved. Then Mr Farnell stepped up to the table to collect his salary. The very quality of the background silence made Jenny sure that some members of the company at least had already suspected Billy's cheating ways. As for her, she was under no illusions that she had made an enemy.

*　*　*

Jenny had been so focused on the Chartwell Players' accounts that she'd almost forgotten there was a world outside her ledger. She was reminded the next day when Lottie came dancing in asking if she was ready to buy the new ribbon for her bonnet.

'And Papa is coming too, for Mrs Jackson says there are rogues here looking for ladies' purses.'

'That is very kind of him, but will he not be bored?'

'He will hand out playbills as we go.'

Jenny's previous experience of big fairs was limited to the annual fair at Bury St Edmunds every October. That was large enough, centred on the marketplace and encompassing the nearby shops, but Midsummer Fair in Cambridge was spread out all over Midsummer Common. There were wharfs along the Cam where barges tied up and offloaded their goods. There were rows of stalls, booths and tents criss-crossing one another in a grid fashion. There was one complete area devoted to earthenware and china, another for horse sales, there were food and haberdashery quarters . . . It was like a small town all to itself. Certainly there seemed to be everything one might wish for on sale; the only difficulty lay in finding it. Jenny bought ribbon, yarn, lengths of material both fancy and plain, and then laid out ninepence on a bag of wiggs warm from the oven, for them all to eat as they went along.

'I love these best of all,' said Lottie happily, licking the sugared caraway seeds from the top of the spiced bun before biting into it with an expression of beatitude on her face.

Will nodded — it was astonishing how he turned up as soon as food was in the offing — and vouchsafed the information to his father that there was a purveyor of leather harnesses just up the row.

Adam looked troubled. 'Can we not make do with what we have?'

'We have done so for months, Pa, but it is wearing very thin.'

'Lead the way, then. And let us hope we get a crowd tonight.'

There were gambling and entertainment booths closer to the centre of the fair. Inside one, Jenny caught sight of Billy Bidens hunched over a hand of cards. Outside another, a man called to customers to see his performing bear.

'Poor creature,' murmured Jenny compassionately. 'He should be curled up in a forest dell, as a cat makes a nest in the stable, not pushed and prodded for man's greed and curiosity.'

Out of the corner of her eye she saw Samuel Obidah, also watching the booth. 'No creature should be chained,' he said softly, and melted away.

As they walked on, Jenny looked at the booths with dissatisfaction. 'We should be giving all these people's audiences *our* playbills. The Chartwell Players are the only comedians here putting on full-length plays. It ought to be obvious that people will get more value for their money by watching us than they will by being robbed in one of these curiosity booths or at a single-act dancing performance.'

'They will be along later,' said Adam in what Jenny couldn't help but feel was a humouring tone. 'Remember also that since Midsummer Fair falls within the town boundaries, we are not licensed to perform pure drama here, so if you do feel moved to mention us, dwell on our songs and dances first and only remark casually that we also provide the theatre-goer with Shakespeare, a farce and a melodrama or pantomime by way of after-piece. As you did to the gentleman the other morning.'

Approaching the horse fair, the lane between the booths grew more crowded. 'You had best hold on to my arm,' said Adam, his eyes sharpening. 'Lottie, take my hand.' In a lower voice he murmured, 'Wherever there are horse sales, there are gypsies. And I am not saying they are all bad by any means, but if there *is* to be trouble, it will involve one of them as sure as eggs are eggs.'

But Jenny could not see any sign of unrest in the businesslike crowd. The Romany clothing interspersed with people's fair-going best gave the place a good-humoured feel. What she did see, with an enormous flutter of her heart, was one of her own tenant farmers bargaining for a horse.

Jenny bent down as if to fix her shoe. Her chest was filled with a confused flurry of hope. Dare she make contact? *Dare she?* She desperately wanted her people to know that she had not abandoned them, but she could not risk calling attention to herself. The fair itself — vendors shouting out wares, people arguing loudly about rival attractions — gave her the answer. She twitched a handbill from Adam's hand. On it, she sketched the bare outlines of a wren.

'Will,' she said casually, her throat nearly closing over, 'go and give this to that lad there with the red hair. He looks as if he could do with some entertainment this afternoon.'

Will looked at her curiously, but did as she bid. As she had hoped, young Rob Starling glanced across. His eyes widened and he tugged at his father's arm. Farmer Starling looked down

145

impatiently, bent to listen to the lad, eyed the playbill then let his contemplative gaze stray in her direction. He gave the smallest of smiles and an imperceptible nod. Jenny smiled at the ground in relief.

10

It wasn't often that Adam took time away from the business of management, but he had to admit it was very pleasant to simply stroll around the fair, with Lottie properly happy again and even Will not too impatient to get to the horse-chandler. He was amused by Jenny's astonishment at all the stalls, and he lost some of his own tautness in seeing the seething Midsummer Common through her eyes. True, he felt his hackles rise when she bought not only ribbons for herself, but also hard-wearing wool for socks and lengths of material evidently designed for his family. But she said placidly that she would keep an account, and he could pay her back when he had the money, and would he please stop spoiling the pleasure of the fair for her.

'I have never seen so much for sale in one place,' she told him. 'It may be quite commonplace for you, so much as you travel around, but I'll wager you were not so blasé and thrifty the first time you were ever in such an abundance of wonders such as this.'

He smiled down at her. 'You are right; I was not. I overspent at the food stall and with the ale-man and fell asleep in the sun behind the bootmaker's tent, where I had fortunately already paid the stallholder to make me a new pair of stout boots.'

'Why fortunate?'

'Because I woke to find my pocket picked, my throat as dry as a drought, and a headache the size of Birmingham threatening to burst from my skull.'

'Oh Adam, no. What did you do?'

'I was so enraged at having been robbed, on top of having a blinding headache, that I charged over to the prize-fighting ring and beat six contenders in succession to win enough of a purse to get me safely to the edge of town, where I could dunk my head in the horse trough and then sleep the clock around.' He eased his neckcloth. 'It taught me several lessons. I've never made that mistake since.'

And it had shown him, once again, that it was imperative he master his anger if he was ever to master himself. At least he hadn't half killed anybody that time. Maybe his fists had been learning restraint of their own accord.

He glanced ruefully down at Jenny's head as she bent to listen to Lottie. There went another uncomfortable memory she'd winkled out of him without even trying. Another rag of shame, hooked up to air out of reach. Perhaps once the raw burn of recollection ebbed, he'd feel lighter for it.

'Did you remember the boots?' asked Will.

Adam met his son's interested eyes, feeling as if the pit of his stomach had been punched. Great heavens, what had he been thinking of, talking so freely before the children? God forbid Will should copy him by example. 'Aye, I retained that much sense, though I'm not sure how. It's not a way of life I'd recommend. I was sore inside and out for days.'

Will nodded thoughtfully, as if tucking the information away. Maybe Adam hadn't done either of them that much of a disservice after all.

He was intensely proud of Will when it came to replacing the worn harness. His son had chosen not the flashiest purveyor, but the one with the best quality goods. When Adam would have cautioned him as to the shortness of their purse, Jenny touched his arm, enjoining silence, and Will himself went for the plainest, most workmanlike tack.

'That's seen some use,' said the craftsman, contemplating the old harness.

'I was going to patch it,' said Will. 'Cut this length out and replace it. But I haven't the skill. Was there more I could have done to look after it?'

The stall holder ran the harness through square, stained hands. 'No, you've done well. It's good to see a boy who understands the value to be got from working the leather. Now, do you have the coin for ready-to-use? Or will you take new leather and work it yourself?'

'I'll work it myself,' said Will immediately. 'The old one will last until I can get the new harness supple enough not to fret the horses.'

'That's a bargain, then.' The crafts-man spat on his hand before clasping Will's to seal it, then looked up at Adam. 'You've got a good lad here.'

Adam felt a sharp ache of pride as he laid his hand on his son's shoulder. 'I know it,' he said. 'I am much blessed. Thank you.'

Will hurried back with his precious harness, leaving the other three to return to the theatre tent more slowly.

'I have sometimes thought,' said Jenny, unerringly putting her finger on another of the things Adam didn't want to think about, 'that Will is more suited to working with horses than acting on the stage.'

A shadow passed over Adam's heart. 'You are right,' he said with a sigh. 'In another year I must take up Susanna and Kit's offer to have the children there, to train Will up for a groom, but just now they are part of me. I need them, though I might not always show it.'

'You wouldn't leave us *behind* at Kydd Court?' said Lottie, wide-eyed and shocked. 'We thought you would stay there too!'

Adam pulled her plait. 'And what would they need with an actor? Never fear, sweetheart, it won't happen yet awhile.' But it was comforting that Lottie at least wanted to be with him. With Will, he could never be sure.

When they got back, Adam watched Jenny tidy her parcels away in the office and begin to make preparations for the evening. She was so brisk and decided. Accustomed to studying the way people moved and talked, he could see all the thought processes involved in her spotting a problem, considering how to fix it, running through the possible solutions, deciding on one and then putting it into action without delay. Very different from the slightly dramatic edge that had characterised Mary's every action. Different again from Lucy's provoking, wide-eyed helplessness. More refreshing too. Of course, both Mary and Lucy were actresses, which Jenny was emphatically not, but it was restful to know he could get on with his own preparations without being required to either praise her or sort out her difficulties himself.

Joe Jackson was on the door with Jenny for today's bill. Once everything was set ready for the performance, Adam kept an unobtrusive eye on her, as he had done ever since she'd joined them. She was more confident about talking to the customers today. One fellow was hanging around instead of finding himself and his lad a place on the benches, but Jenny didn't seem at all ill at ease; she just chatted to him cheerfully until he went through.

★ ★ ★

When Jenny stretched out on her pallet that night, she had plenty to think about. According to Farmer Starling, the new earl had put it about that she had gone away on a visit, leaving the management of her estate in his hands. Relieved that there was no hue and cry out for her, and that her riding horse remained unmolested in Farmer Starling's stable, she still fretted about Cousin Vincent's intentions towards her land. While the plays were on, she had written another letter to Mr Tweedie asking him to please send someone to Rooke Hall as a matter of urgency to look after her interests. She'd then slipped it to her tenant for posting.

Farmer Starling had commented stolidly that at least he'd be able to find her if it proved necessary and that he would let her other tenant farmer know, but that the secret of her whereabouts would go no further. All the same, she could not help worrying. And either her fidgeting disturbed Lottie or (which was more likely) the number of sugared buns consumed that day caused the child to stir restlessly.

'Mama,' she whimpered in her sleep. 'Mama . . . '

Jenny felt for Lottie's hand, but Adam was before her. 'Mama is watching over you,' he soothed. 'Go back to sleep.'

'Mama,' sobbed Lottie.

Jenny could not bear it. She sat up and reached across, fetching up against Adam. 'Hush, darling. All's well.'

Lottie turned towards her voice. Jenny wriggled closer, balancing so as not to touch the warm solidity of Adam's shirtless chest more than was necessary, curving her arm around Lottie's shuddering shoulders. 'There, now. Go to sleep.'

'Papa,' murmured Lottie.

Adam leant forward, leaning around Jenny to stroke his daughter's head. 'I'm here, sweetheart.'

Lottie quietened, breathed more

deeply, relaxed again into sleep.

'I think I have cramp,' said Jenny after a supremely uncomfortable moment when she expected Adam to move back to his own bedroll and he didn't.

'Hmm? Oh, that's awkward. She usually needs five or ten minutes before I can be certain she won't rouse again. Where does it hurt?'

'My, er, hip,' she said hastily, naming the least embarrassing place closest to the site of the cramp.

'Is this better?'

Jenny froze in shock as his capable fingers kneaded her hip through the cotton of her nightgown. The tension made her cramp worse and she emitted a gasp.

'Ah, no, I see. How about this?' His fingers inched sideways over her buttock.

'Yes,' said Jenny, flustered. Thankfully, she eased her leg into a different position. It was fortunate that it was dark so he could not see how extremely embarrassed she was. 'That is much better. Thank you.'

'In the old days we often used to present tableaux and had to hold positions for several minutes at a time. One becomes familiar with common cramp points.'

And he was an actor, of course, accustomed to casual contact in the course of his work. What seemed a lot to her would mean very little to him. 'Are you happy, Adam?' said Jenny abruptly. 'Are you happy in this life?'

'Happy?' She felt him shrug, his skin moving against her nightgown. 'I bring pleasure to people, my children are fed and clothed. It is as much as most folk aspire to.'

But how bleak he sounded. How far away. There was more to life than simply existing, else why did he glow so when in another character's skin on the stage?

She was aware of Adam's warmth against her back, of the solid safety of his body. This was very different to yesterday's triumphant hug at getting the accounts straightened out. Unversed in the ways of love, Jenny was nevertheless abundantly sure that if she leant into him, if she turned her head to lay her cheek against his chest, he would see it as an invitation and, embrace or reject, it would move their relationship beyond where it was comfortable. The complications from *that* would be enormous. Accordingly she murmured, 'I think Lottie is quieter now, don't you? You have more experience than I.'

There was the very smallest pause before he shifted gently away. 'Thank you,' he said.

She looked up and met his eyes in the dim light. Everything he had said or hadn't said over the course of these few weeks coalesced in her head. She wanted to tell him there was always a choice. She wanted to tell him fighting wasn't always wrong, and running away wasn't always cowardly. She wanted to say that staying was sometimes the worst decision of all. Instead she touched his arm, wordless, and slid back into her own bedroll again.

When Jenny went upstairs to change for dinner, she found the young African nursery maid in her chamber looking slyly malicious.

'The master says I'm to see to you from now on. I used to be the mistress's maid. I wasn't always in the nursery. I know how to dress a lady and make her look pretty.'

Jenny's unease intensified. 'Thank him for his consideration, Bella, but I already have a maid and do not require another.'

'You must. He says so. The mistress was very fond of me. She couldn't do without me.'

'I daresay. But I am happy with my own woman. You may return to the nursery.'

The girl left, but when hot water was brought up for Jenny to wash with, she heard sobs and an odd thudding from her cousin's suite of rooms. And when she called into the nursery later to wish

Eddie goodnight, Bella's face was bruised.

'How did this happen?' she asked, concerned. 'Shall I fetch you a salve?'

Bella eyed her with sullen satisfaction. 'You sent me away. This was to teach me not to fail next time.'

'My cousin did this to you?' Jenny was profoundly shocked.

'And more.' Bella's eyes darted around, then she seized Jenny's arm and pulled her behind a screen. She hauled up her print dress to show a pattern of welts down her naked back and legs. 'And then he took me,' she hissed. 'He said you'd get a taste of the same if you crossed him too often.'

11

It was during their second week at Cambridge that the letters came for Jenny: one delivered by her other tenant farmer, and one by the head groom from Penfold Lodge who had apparently travelled the sixteen miles to Midsummer Fair for the express purpose of checking over the horses in young Will's care.

Will coloured bright red when Mr Flood stopped majestically by the theatre tent on his way to the horse fair. He gabbled the rest of his speeches with far more animation than normal in his haste to finish the rehearsal. Jenny caught Adam's impatient eye and motioned to Flood to move out into the entrance so as not to embarrass the lad further. No one seeing the incident — as the whole company did — would be in any danger of interpreting the gesture as anything other than Jenny saving the rehearsal from further interruption.

My dearest Jenny, wrote Aunt Sophy, *we are very well, and very well pleased to have news of you from both Mrs Kydd and Mr Tweedie. Your cousin has been here several times demanding to see you, but appears now to have accepted that you are not within. He has set men to watch the house and imagines he has gained the confidence of one of the stable lads. Pray take care, my dear. I could wish you had chosen a more conventional solution to your problem, but I can quite see you do not want any of your friends accused of kidnap or suspected of concealing you. As we know, the Earl has a very nasty temper indeed. We get on very well here, and Mrs Penfold has taught me a new knitting stitch.*

The second letter was from Mr Tweedie, and rather different in tone.

I am grieved to say that the description of your relative's actions comes as no surprise to me, having made enquiries as I told you I would into the manner of his running his shipping business. I have not been able to obtain details of the working practices on his plantations in Jamaica, but I fear it would be a similar tale there. Incidentally, my junior partner Mr Congreve caught sight of the earl briefly when he visited these chambers and swears he knows him in connection with something unsavoury, but cannot at present bring it to mind. (I have told him this is NOT WHAT I EXPECT in a partner. A man of the law's memory is his greatest asset.)

Even so, I cannot express too strongly my dismay at your present method of concealing yourself from his notice. Surely you have friends with whom you can pass a blameless few months until your majority is attained? This travelling life cannot be what you are used to. If news of the escapade ever reaches the polite world, I fear your reputation will be quite ruined. However, it is so very unconventional an act that I daresay no one will believe it, and so I shall strenuously suggest if word ever comes to my ears.

As to your tenants, I have passed on your instructions and suggested that a certain slowness and stupidity on their part should deflect too pressing an interest in their affairs by your cousin. I regret that I cannot visit Rooke Hall again so soon. I did so after receiving your first note, but the earl claims that you are presently away on a visit, and he has shown me a letter giving him full power to deal with your estate. On my remarking that I was familiar with your hand and expressing my surprise at you employing a scribe for those instructions, he informed me that you had been indisposed at the time. I then wondered aloud that you would go visiting when ill and he snapped that *it was for the good of your health. I do not wish to provoke him too far, lest he engage some other firm of solicitors and I lose what perilous influence I have over the estate. I believe I have shown enough teeth for him to see that while riding roughshod over the truth may have been sufficient in Jamaica, it assuredly will not do in England.*

Jenny tucked the letters away with some sadness. They would likely comprise the only news of home that she would receive for a considerable time. She had been lucky, seeing Farmer Starling at the horse sales. She couldn't count on another occurrence like that. The fair was drawing to a close, and then the Chartwell Players would be off in a new direction, never staying anywhere for longer than a few days.

She had already given Mr Flood a verbal message for Aunt Sophy. She wouldn't risk speaking to him again. Mr Tweedie might think his mild words had given her cousin pause, but Jenny knew to what lengths the man would go in order to get hold of her. It was better this way, safer for all concerned. All the same, she hadn't reckoned on the wrench she would feel at being briefly reunited with her own world and then having to shut it out again.

Fortunately, Lottie came dancing into the office before Jenny could give herself over to a thorough mope, saying the rehearsal was over and she had been good and had Mr Flood happened to bring anything with him from the Penfold Lodge kitchen?

'You had best ask your brother,' replied Adam, following her. 'If I am not mistaken, it was he whom the groom came to see.' His eyes met Jenny's over Lottie's flying braids. 'I have never seen him play better. I could wish I attracted the same devotion.'

'You think he was acting for Mr Flood's benefit? I thought rather that he was racing to get to the end of the scene so he could go to the stables.'

Adam gave her a rueful smile. 'You do not need to dress up your words for me. I know full well where his heart lies. And yes, I shall do something about it. The look on his face today decided me.'

Jenny crossed the room to link her arm quickly in his, to give him the reassurance of touch. 'I believe you are right, but I do not think you need be in too much of a hurry to lose him. Simply talking to Will about the various possibilities in front of him, and both of you discussing together what he might like to do, would work a power of good.'

He stared down at her, puzzlement in his face. Jenny let Lottie tug them outside, stopping only to secure the canvas divider.

'Think back,' she said softly once they were walking again. 'At ten years old, did you imagine you had any future beyond what the adults in your world had mapped out for you?'

A startled jolt ran down his arm, giving her his answer.

'Then why should you think it is any different for Will?' she continued. 'His whole life has been travelling and the theatre. He might not realise he has a choice. Forgive me, but he may not perceive you would allow — nay, encourage — him to make his own decision as to which of life's paths to follow.'

'So I am a failure as a father as well as a husband?' said Adam bitterly.

'No!' She gave his arm a shake. 'Stop this, Adam. You are a very good father. You have kept yourself together for your children in the face of your grief. You have kept their way of life intact and given them the comfort of continuity. But I would suggest it is time to be a family again. *Talk* to them, not just tell them. You and Will are very alike, but you are older, wiser, stronger and more experienced in the world than your son. All those things should help Will, not hinder him.'

He was walking unthinkingly at her pace now, measured and thoughtful, his eyes on Lottie skipping ahead of them.

'You make a valid point,' he said slowly. 'If I cannot read him, how should he to be expected to read me? Thank you.'

★   ★   ★

When they returned from their stroll about the fair, Jenny went into the office to remove her cloak. And froze. Someone had been in here during their absence. The ledger was aslant on the desk. The pile of mending on top of the chest was not in the same order as she had left it. There was a fold of material showing underneath the lid of the chest itself. She spread her arms to stop the others following her in, her eyes taking note of each anomaly. The bedrolls had been disturbed. Her valises were askew. One of the drawers in the cabinet had not been shut properly. Anger flooded her. How dare they!

'We have had visitors,' she said in a tight voice.

Adam, she was gratified to see, didn't doubt her for a second. 'I'll ask if anyone saw anything.'

Jenny listened. She heard Mrs Jackson say that they had only got back five minutes ago themselves. The Furnells were evidently out. Further back in the main tent, there was a rumble of male conversation.

Adam reappeared. 'Nothing has been moved in the Jacksons' dressing room. Mrs Jackson thinks she saw the whisk of cloth across the entrance as they returned, but Lucy and Grace weren't looking. Apparently they'd fallen into conversation with a very nice gentleman who had admired Lucy's acting and who had proved to be an actor himself, with the Norwich Company. The girls had been too engrossed in watching him as he departed to pay attention to anything else. Billy and Chas have been playing cards on the stage all afternoon and haven't noticed anything out of the ordinary.'

Billy Bidens and his brother Chas. Why was Jenny not surprised to hear that those two were the ones who had supposedly been guarding the tent today? Her lips thinned.

Adam crossed to the chest. 'Has anything been taken?' he asked.

'No,' said Jenny. 'Everything not locked has been looked through, I believe, but it seems our visitor was disturbed.'

'As well it is wages day tomorrow; we will be rid of most of the coin then. I'll take another walk around the tent now to make sure all is secure.'

Once he had gone, Jenny sat down, thinking grimly. Billy had been in here looking for money, she didn't doubt it for a second. The man was a gambler and a showy dresser, and not always as lucky as he would like. She grimaced, thinking of his hands rifling through her small clothes, then wrapped her arms around her waist, feeling the reassurance of the pockets of money she kept under her gown. She had devised the pockets as the safest way of carrying her own money with her when she fled home. Since they had been at Midsummer Fair, she had taken the precaution of adding the Chartwell Players' store to them during the day. It looked as if she would be wise to continue the practice.

She sighed. She had little with her worth stealing in the way of possessions, and theft of money was in no way as serious as threats towards her person, but it would behove her to keep a more stringent lookout nevertheless. It seemed as though her hopes of leading a more carefree existence for a few months were at an end. At least it was only money in jeopardy this time, not worse. At least here she did not have to worry about potential accidents to her person. That, after all, was one of the reasons why she had come away.

★ ★ ★

The message had been delivered via Bella. Jenny and Aunt Sophy were to dine by themselves that evening. The earl had visitors from London to do with his business, common fellows not suitable for the company of ladies. Jenny didn't mind at all; she was only surprised at her cousin's unexpected delicacy of feeling.

The meal was served by one of the youngest of Cousin Vincent's servants, a young man who Jenny had noticed previously as being clearly unhappy in this cold, damp new country.

'What is this, Barnaby?' she asked as he ladled an unfamiliar soup into the bowl in front of her.

His face lit up. 'A spiced chicken soup from my country. It is very good. Massa ordered it special for tonight.'

So his own chef would have made it, not the Rooke Hall resident cook. More friction in the kitchen; and whether it was all eaten or not, somebody's feelings would be hurt. Jenny sighed and covered her reflections with a smile for Barnaby's benefit.

Aunt Sophy had a spoonful and made a face. She disliked anything spicy. Jenny managed half a bowl, but the dish had an unpleasant aftertaste.

Barnaby's eyes gleamed, seeing how little they had eaten. Jenny hid a smile, guessing that the tureen would be empty by the time he delivered it back to the kitchen.

It was comfortable, eating on their own, talking over the small doings of their day the way they always used to but which Cousin Vincent stigmatised as trivial nonsense. Jenny could wish every meal might be the same. She was all the more annoyed, therefore, to be taken with stomach cramps later, resulting in a private session voiding her stomach. She was completely well again by the morning, but lamented the waste of a quiet, uninterrupted evening.

In the nursery the next day, there was an underlying sombreness, and Ruth was red-eyed. Upon Jenny's enquiring the reason, she said, 'Young Barnaby was taken ill in the night and died. Retched his heart out, just like the mistress did on the ship. It's a sad day.'

Bella eyed Jenny in an avid manner. 'You seem pale, miss.'

174

Jenny might make conversation out of trivialities with Aunt Sophy, but she was far from stupid. Her mind had gone instantly from her disturbed evening to Barnaby's enthusiasm over the highly spiced taste-masking soup. The soup that her cousin had ordered specially on a day when she and her aunt were eating in isolation from the rest of the household. 'Naturally I am sad and shocked about Barnaby, Bella,' she said in a voice of light reproof. But when she sat down to read Eddie a story, her legs were very shaky indeed under the cover of her long skirts.

12

Midsummer Fair was packing up. The walkways between the stalls were all shouting and confusion. Lottie had begged to see the barges being loaded, so Jenny had gone with her. The wharves, permanent and makeshift, were crowded with organised bustle. Jenny and Lottie stood on the bank watching the colourful, noisy proceedings.

There were a lot of other people watching the loading; people who, like them, were waiting until Midsummer Common was less congested before packing their own wagons and leaving. Someone jostled Jenny just as a crate of pottery fell with an ear-jerking crash on the nearest wharf. Jenny's attention, like most of the crowd, was immediately captured by the pot-seller letting out a barrage of furious screams and curses at the luckless porter who had let the crate slip.

Not everybody was distracted, though. As her head turned towards the wharf, Jenny felt a brutal, deliberate shove between her shoulder blades. Caught off balance, her boots slipped on the muddy bank and she tumbled headlong into the Cam. Her yell of outrage was cut off by a mouthful of grey-brown river as the waters closed over her head. Unable to breathe, she realised in terror that she was still sinking; that the weight of the money belt under her gown was pulling her relentlessly down. The last thing she heard before she blacked out was Lottie's piercing, high-pitched scream.

★ ★ ★

The first indication Adam had that something was wrong was Lottie's scream. Their effects were all corded and ready for the road, and he was impatient to be off, but there was no point striking the Chartwell Players' tent until the area became less of a squeeze. He had determined instead to check that Jenny and

Lottie were safe in the crowd, when the urgency of his daughter's penetrating yell gave his feet wings. Blood pounding in his veins, he powered in the direction of her voice, pushing folk unceremoniously out of the way. What had happened? Why was Jenny not taking care of her? Had Lottie fallen under a cart? Been abducted? His heart almost burst with relief when he made her out running towards him, her braids flying, with tears wet on her face.

'Jenny!' she screamed, grabbing his hand and pulling him back the way she had come. 'Jenny's drowning in the river!'

Adam scooped her up without further thought and ran for the wharf, shoving through the gaps in the press of people. It was easy to see where to head for. A great knot of spectators were gathered by the bank, shouting encouragement. One man had a billhook and another had a pole, prodding into the mud. Adam didn't even stop to consider. He thrust Lottie at the nearest person, tore off his boots and jumped headlong into the water where a billow of yellow material and a small patch of bubbles indicated Jenny's position.

The water was muddy and noxious. Adam forced his eyes to stay open as he plunged down. The Cam was not deep here, but deep enough if one didn't swim and was unaware of river safety. He saw an unformed mass of yellow beneath him, got a hand into a fold of material, and pulled hard as he struck out for the surface.

Jenny weighed an enormous amount, far more than he would have expected. He hauled her against him as they came up into the air. There was something lumpy around her waist. Her head lolled. She wasn't even spluttering, clearly unconscious. He had to get whatever she had taken in expelled from her as fast as possible. 'Come on,' he muttered. 'Come on.'

A cheer went up, and hands reached down to pull them both ashore.

'No,' shouted Adam. 'You'll wear away the bank and make it worse.'

There was a shallow inlet fifty yards down. He forged through the water towards it, knowing speed was essential.

Once on the bank, he laid Jenny on her side and started rocking her without delay. A lump on her temple showed that the fellow wielding the pole had hindered rather than helped her plight. What if it had been fatal? Dear God, he wanted to kill somebody himself, but there was no time. Rock, rock, rock, panic in his heart, and on his lips a silent prayer.

Water trickled from Jenny's mouth; then with a gasping sob, she retched uncontrollably.

Adam felt a great weight of anxiety slough off his back. She was alive. Her eyes were fluttering, she was breathing, even if she was far from cognisant of anything around her. 'Come on,' he said. 'More. Choke it all up. Come on.'

She retched again, and then some more. A tinge of colour appeared in her face. 'See, Lottie,' said Adam to his sobbing daughter. 'She is getting better.

Soon she will be well again. Be a brave girl and mop your eyes now. I'll need you in a moment.'

Once all the river water was gone from Jenny's lungs, Adam carried her to the theatre tent, feeling his legs start to go heavy and his wet garments drag at his limbs. This was his danger point. He knew full well it was only the rush of movement keeping him going; that as soon as he stopped he would be drained, just as when the euphoria of performance left him. The trick was to keep up the emotional force until he could afford to relax. So he summoned his old rage against the world and roared his way into the tent, calling for towels to be unpacked and hot water to be conjured from somewhere, all the time knowing he needed to find out what was wrapped around Jenny so heavily and bulkily and *not* wanting anyone else to know about it just yet.

'My leather bag, Lottie,' he said urgently under the hubbub. 'I need it now.'

Jenny's dress had been ripped at some point during the rescue. Adam glimpsed a thick petticoat through the gaping tear and a row of pockets attached to a fabric belt tied around her waist. He didn't know what it was, but he trusted her implicitly. If she'd hidden something on her person, she would want it to stay hidden, not be discovered by a well-meaning Mrs Jackson, who was even now bearing down on him with her voluble daughters.

Will thrust his way through the crowd at a run, presumably alerted by the noise. Lottie had found the leather bag and was darting back to her father's side. 'Knife, Will,' said Adam quickly.

His son immediately passed across his precious blade. Adam sliced through Jenny's fabric to one side of the sodden knot and passed the knife back to Will without anyone seeing. Under cover of lowering Jenny to the ground, he tugged at the hidden pockets and stuffed the whole length of them into the leather bag. It was only when he heard the chink of coins that he realised what in part the contents must be. Jenny had nearly drowned safeguarding the Chartwell Players' treasury. She could have died. Adam was more shocked by this — and by the immense, unexpected wrench his heart gave at the thought of it — than by the whole fact of the accident happening in the first place. He reeled in utter surprise, letting Mrs Jackson take charge.

Will tugged his arm, pulling him towards the end of the tent. 'You must get dry too, Pa,' he said.

Adam felt the smooth leather of the drawstring bag gripped in his fist. He felt the weight of it, mirroring the clammy drag of his clothes. He focused on his son's gruff words, on his daughter's frightened face. God help him, he needed to be strong still. He couldn't give way; he couldn't afford to collapse and give his emotions their much-needed release.

'Clothes, Lottie. Will, I'll need your

help to strip me of this lot. I daresay my boots are long gone.'

'I brought them from the river,' said Lottie, her teeth chattering now with the aftermath of shock. 'Is Jenny all right?'

'She will be soon, and all due to you, raising the alarm so quick. She is lucky indeed to have made such a friend. You did well, sweetheart, very well indeed.'

Lottie's lip wobbled as she pulled breeches and a shirt out of the trunk for him. 'I will get Jenny a gown out too. Billy Bidens was by the bank, but he wouldn't help. He said he couldn't swim and turned away. You saved her.'

Adam was towelling himself dry now, arms working, keeping the blood flowing in his veins, bringing his leaden, numb skin back to life. 'I did. How is Mrs Jackson doing with her, Lottie? We must strike the tent, finish loading up and make space for Jenny in the wagon with a blanket to keep her warm, for she'll not be up to walking. Is the press of folk less out there yet, Will?'

He had stepped outside himself, he realised, just as he had at the moment when the first shovel of earth fell on Mary's coffin; and he knew above all things that he had to get away from Kydd Court and away from the weight of guilt upon his soul. Now he felt light-headed and lucid, and saw his way clear as day laid out before him. He must keep moving, keep working, and there was nothing to be gained from staying here amongst the last remnants of the fair.

Two things stood out above all in his mind. Another good week's takings would see the company arrears straight; Jenny had said so when they were dealing with the wages this time. The Newmarket July Meeting was imminent. A racing week was far from an ideal environment for the ladies in his troupe, but it *was* a lucrative source of income with the right plays and songs. Adam was sick of debt. He was sick of the constant reminders of his inadequacy. Just recently, it seemed to him that he'd been failing all his life. He didn't care about his own circumstances, but he loved his children, and he was desperate to stand clear and no longer have the whole financial weight of responsibility of the company on his shoulders. A week amongst the open-handed race-goers at Newmarket would see to that.

The other reason was Jenny. Without at all meaning to — without even realising when it had happened — he had grown to care for her, and he was damned if he was losing one more person because of his own shortcomings. To put it purely and simply, there was a doctor in Newmarket he had faith in who had several times treated Mary. If Jenny was slow to recover, Adam wanted to be near someone who could help her sooner rather than later.

* * *

Jenny was aware by the jolting of her whole body that she was alive and not

186

in that desperate green-brown place where water invaded her lungs and pushed all the air out of her. She was lying on folds of material, with more close-packed around her, but there was a weak light seeping in from under her lashes, so she was not yet in the grave. She did not seem able to open her eyes further, nor move her limbs even the tiniest amount. As it happened, they felt so heavy, and her head throbbed to such an extent, that she didn't wish to move at all. She fretted, now hot, now icily cold, not knowing what was amiss. Far off, she heard Adam's voice and was insensibly calmed. He was a comfortable rumble of sound that harmonised the other noises about her and made the world safe. She listened to his words rising and falling as he talked to Will and Lottie, and strove to stay awake, trying not to descend back into her sweat-soaked, murderous memories.

★　★　★

She was cantering across the Prior's Ground towards the copse at the far end. Rain had kept her within doors for several days, and her mare was restive. The groom was some way behind her. Not that a groom was necessary, when she knew the whole estate as well as she knew her own bedchamber; but there had been something in Cousin Vincent's manner at breakfast when he had quizzed her on how she intended to spend her day that had made her think it might be as well to be accompanied this morning.

The lanes between the fields were soft with the constant rain of the past few weeks, but at least it was dry for now, even if the clouds were low and mid-grey. The long-ago monks of the Prior's Ground had worked to make their demesne a place of beauty. The features of the land remained, even if the Priory itself had long gone. There was a copse set upon a grassy knoll, an obvious goal beckoning at the end of the vista. On the flat stretch just before it, Jenny could let the mare have her head. The horse knew it and gathered speed; but just as Jenny was about to give the signal to go faster, she saw movement behind the trees.

She wheeled in alarm. No one should be there that she knew of. She called to her groom to rally to her, just as a cloud of birds erupted skywards and a man on horseback burst out from behind a thorny shrub and made off towards the denser thickets in the woodland on Rooke Hall land.

Jenny slowed, her heart pounding, heading for the point where she had first seen movement. What she found made the breath freeze in her throat and caused her to nearly slide from the saddle in horror. A thin cord had been stretched between two trees on either side of the natural opening into the copse. It would have been invisible at speed and would have caught her horse just below the chest. Jenny herself would likely have broken her neck in the resultant fall.

Staring at the deadly twine, her conviction crystallised. She must get away from here, and soon.

★ ★ ★

Jenny seemed to have been in the jolting wagon forever. Memories came and haunted her and went. The throbbing in her head intensified. Once or twice, Lottie scrambled up beside her and held a cup of cooled water to her lips. Through it all, Adam's voice held her together, reassuring her subconsciously that she wasn't back in the nightmare round of watching what she ate or where she rode or trod. He must have spent the whole journey walking alongside the wagon, talking to the men about plays to put on next, discussing the playbills to be commissioned, checking on the state of the animal foodstuff stores with Will. Jenny couldn't follow what he was saying. It was enough to know he was there.

They stopped for a longer period.

She dozed fitfully, soothed by the sounds of purposeful bustle. She was aware of things being taken out of the wagon, but didn't connect this with having arrived anywhere until Lottie once more climbed up to cradle her head and she found herself being eased into Adam's arms. She made an attempt at protest, as being raised up made her head swim and her stomach unstable.

'Hush, sweetheart,' murmured Adam in her ear. 'It is only to lie you down in the barn. As soon as the cooking fire is going, you shall have some of Mary's fever tea. All will be well, I promise.'

All will be well. The words settled in Jenny's soul. She laid her head on his shoulder and didn't struggle further. Once in her familiar bedroll, she let Lottie bathe her forehead and tuck the coverings around her.

'Get better,' whispered the little girl anxiously. 'We need you.'

The worry in the child's voice pierced Jenny's passive acceptance of her state as nothing else could have done. She forced herself to answer coherently. 'I will,' she said, and as she heard herself speak, the world shifted itself sideways into focus. The miasma of illness was replaced by something sharper and more tangible. 'I will,' she repeated, and this time she slept properly.

She woke several times during the night to hear the familiar breathing of Adam and the children around her, making her feel safe and soothed and fixed in her own skin again. The first time she stirred, Adam was awake and helped her sip a warm, faintly scented infusion.

'Thank you,' she said, marvelling at how comfortable she was with him. It didn't feel in the least strange for him to be cradling her in a raised position. It felt wholly natural. Being nursed dispensed with all awkwardness. She hated being out of control of her body like this, but almost regretted the return to formality which better health would bring. *I could live with Adam forever,* she thought drowsily. *I would be safe forever. Held like this forever. Loved forever.*

The fever had one more bout of bad dreams in store before daylight, a confused chase through dark passages and over crumbling bridges with the menace of her cousin constantly behind her. She awoke from them too suddenly, sweat-soaked and with palpitating heart, but, she realised with utter relief, clear in her mind at last.

'Are you better?' asked Adam. He was dressed and sitting at the desk, but there were shadows under his eyes.

'I believe I am,' said Jenny in a thankful voice. 'Although I might need help to the . . . '

She had to lean on his arm as they made their way slowly to the door of the barn. Her back felt horribly bruised from the force of the blow that had pushed her into the river. She would have to tell Adam of that. She faltered for a moment at the thought of laying yet another burden of care on this man.

'Can you manage?' he said. 'Should I wake Lottie?'

She wouldn't disturb him with the truth just yet. She would allow herself the luxury of a quarter of an hour revelling in the fact that she was still alive, she was well, and that after yesterday's endless journey, she was yet another day's travel further from her cousin. 'I can manage,' she said.

Adam eased open the barn door on to a dank, overcast dawn, but the unwelcome prospect of more rain wasn't what stopped Jenny in her tracks and rooted her wooden pattens to the ground. She took one appalled look at the vista, at the wide sky and the pattern of the trees and hedgerows that she knew from a thousand, thousand visits, and turned to Adam, dismay flooding her whole body.

'This is Newmarket,' she whispered, hardly able to force the words from a throat swollen with terror.

'It is the July Meeting next week.' His

eyes were puzzled, his voice defensive. 'I know the racing gentlemen can be raucous and overly familiar and very often drunk, but that is why we are staying here on the site, to keep you women safe. The takings are always good, Jenny, even though it is only a three-day meeting. I think to do three racing days, and then one more for the townsfolk before moving on. You did say a good week would see my debts to the players clear.'

Jenny stared at him in horror. This was what came of taking the easy passage. She should have told him all, right from the start. 'I believe it will, but I cannot stay to see it.' She turned her head and pointed with a shaking hand across the scant yards of grass separating the barn from the road to Fordham. 'Adam, four miles that way is my home . . . and my cousin, who wants me dead.'

13

Jenny sat in the chair at the end of the office. Across the smallest of spaces from her, Adam raked his fingers through his hair, then leant forward on his stool to take her hands. They kept their voices low, mindful of the sleeping children.

'Tell me,' said Adam simply.

Jenny was glad of the warmth from his hands. She had wrapped herself in her good Norwich shawl, but she seemed to be cold all the way to her core. 'I tried to explain when I first came to you. You thought I was jesting, and to my shame it was easier to let you go on thinking that. When my father died, the bulk of the estate passed to a distant cousin in Jamaica, whom we had never met. The smaller, non-entailed part came to me. It was my father's way of providing for me. My cousin, however, has now come to England to claim his inheritance, and wants my portion of the land too because it gives him access to the watercourse so he can irrigate his own farms more easily. If I die before my twenty-fifth birthday, that is exactly what he will get.'

'And you thought yourself in such danger from him that you ran away?' Adam sounded incredulous, as well he might. 'Have you confirmation of his intent, then?'

Jenny swallowed and met his eyes squarely. 'There have been two occasions on which I was lucky to live, and a number of other times when an accident might have occurred, though I have no actual proof, only circumstantial evidence. From my knowledge of his temperament, from his attitude, his looks, past actions and manner of talking, I am in no doubt at all of my cousin's design.'

'Could you not confide in his wife? Have you no friends to stay with?

Susanna would surely give you refuge.'

'Certainly she would, and it was the first thing she suggested, as did Caroline Rothwell and Louisa Fortune. But I will not bring my friends into danger from either him or the law if he cries kidnap. As for my cousin's wife, she died on the voyage to England. He evinces no distress at her loss.'

'He is a widower? Then why does he not wed you and get the land that way?'

Jenny winced at the brutality of the question, but answered quietly. 'He may have had some thoughts of it, but it is better for him if I expire before the limits on the bequest do. On my marriage *or* my twenty-fifth birthday, the Prior's Ground comes directly to me in trust for my lifetime and to my heirs thereafter. I imagine even Cousin Vincent baulks at the death of a second wife in as many months — and at the altar itself too, because I assure you the first thing I would sign on becoming the Countess of Harwood would be my will, leaving the Prior's Ground to any person at all, provided they are unconnected to him.'

Adam started back. 'Countess . . . ?'

Jenny felt like crying. 'Oh, Adam, pray do not look at me like that. My father's was only a very minor earldom and my small farms bring in enough to keep me comfortable, no more. I do not even have a home to live in, not until the Prior's House is fully repaired. At present, half of it is still crumbling walls and makeshift floors.'

He bowed his head. 'And are you really Jenny Castle?' he asked with a touch of bitterness.

'Here, I am. In another life I was Lady Jane Rooke. It is not quite a lie, Adam. I have always been Jenny to my family and friends. And I *am* well acquainted with Susanna. I met her through Caroline Rothwell, whom I befriended at school. I intended telling you the whole as soon as I arrived, but you were troubled and I knew I could help and . . . and it has been such a strain since my father died that I longed

to be anonymous, of no account . . . '
Jenny broke off, feeling her thoughts
tangle. 'I have been very comfortable as
Jenny Castle.'

He stood up, with the remote look on
his face that she had sometimes seen
before. 'You say you would not put
your friends in danger. Why then did
you come to the Chartwell Players? To
me?'

'The honest answer is because
Cousin Vincent would not expect such
a thing. Nor would anybody. I daresay
my poor Mr Tweedie very near had a
seizure when he received my first note
telling him of my whereabouts. But I
also came to you because Susanna said
you needed me. It was not to imperil
you and yours, you must never think
that. I told you what I wanted, Adam.
To be busy. To be helpful. To live a
normal life again.' She paused. 'To
forget. To be safe.'

He gave a short laugh. 'Which you
patently aren't. Tumbling into rivers fit
to drown. You are likely to do your

cousin's work for him.'

Jenny took another breath. This was also going to hurt him, but she saw no way of softening it. 'I did not tumble. I was pushed. Of a certainty, pushed. I can still feel the imprint of a hand on my back. I daresay were you to look, you would see a bruise.'

He stared at her in consternation. 'Pushed? Your cousin cannot have been at Midsummer Fair, else he would surely have tracked you here already!'

'I did not say it was my cousin. I believe the shove into the Cam was out of spite, a lucky chance taken with the desire to see me get a drenching.' She paused. 'Billy Bidens has no love for me, Adam.'

'You think it was Billy? Lottie said he was in the crowd but would not help when she asked. I will discharge him for that if for nothing else.'

'Can you manage the bigger plays without him? He will claim innocence and I cannot prove anything, Adam, though I do believe it to be true.'

He made an impatient gesture. 'Then what am I to do? I cannot be always watching him.'

'It is not fair on your troupe to foment discord within it or to bring danger upon you all should my cousin discover my whereabouts. He is quite likely to burn down the barn while we sleep, simply to get rid of me. You are right. I will leave.' As she said the words, a weight of hopelessness settled on her heart.

'You will not!' Adam's voice rose.

'Hush,' she said, flapping her hand. They both turned, but the children slept on, undisturbed.

'You will not!' Adam's voice rose.

'You will not,' he repeated in a low, fierce tone, griping her hands. 'You came to us for employment and invisibility. You may have that still.'

'Adam, how? You must see that I cannot take the entrance money at the performances here. Even if most of the audience are from outside Newmarket, there will be sufficient local people who know me to raise any number of alarms.'

He brushed that away. 'You do not have to take the money. Joe and his father will do it, and you may count it in here out of sight and enter it in the ledger as usual. I shall say none of the women in the company are to be exposed to the racing fraternity's ebullience during what is well known to be a high-spirited few days away from the steadying influence of their own families. We have taken such measures before.'

'Thank you,' said Jenny in a whisper. 'Then Billy will also remain in the company for now and I will continue with your accounts. Oh . . . ' Her hands shot to her waist. The money pockets! She had been wearing them when she fell in the Cam. She remembered her sick dread when she realised they were pulling her down. Where were they? Had they become untied? Had she lost the Chartwell Players' treasury in the Midsummer Common mud? Adam would surely hate her now.

He crossed to his strongbox and withdrew from it a leather bag. 'I did not know what was yours and what was ours,' he said, handing it to her. 'I am humbled, Jenny.'

The money was safe. 'Oh, thank goodness. I would have paid you back had it been lost,' she said, hardly hearing him. She drew out the still-damp pockets, thanking the Lord that she had wrapped the folding money in waxed felt against the rain. 'Be sure I will not be going near any more rivers while wearing this.'

'It should not have been necessary at all.'

Jenny looked up at Adam in surprise. 'But it is safer to keep large sums out of sight, and with everything corded and ready to go, I did not want to take the risk of your boxes being loaded on to the wrong cart and the takings lost.'

He caught her to him, his hands hard on her arms. '*I* should have seen to it. *Me*. Jenny, your safety means more to me than money. I can do recitations in the street for money.' He shut his eyes as if drawing strength from somewhere, and then opened them again. 'Listen to me ranting while you are still ill. You would think it was me who had been knocked on the head. Jenny, I thank you for your forethought, but you *must* let me be responsible. You must. Mary kept things from me with the best of intentions, and she died because I didn't know there was anything to look for. I will not lose anyone else because I do not have sufficient knowledge to prevent it.'

He meant it. He was cross with her. The knowledge was blinding. 'Forgive me,' she said, rushing headlong into speech likewise because it was so important for him to know this. 'It was not a deliberate act, I promise. I have been too long accustomed to making my own decisions because there was no one else to ask. I didn't think. I am sorry.' She ran out of words. Their bodies were close together, their hearts beating in time. She had never felt so much on the brink of something irrevocable. 'I don't know what to say,' she whispered.

He drew her even closer, pressed her head against his breast, holding her for three, maybe four, precious, wonderful heartbeats. 'Nor do I,' he said on a thread of breath, 'but I do know that I cannot well do without you . . . and I cannot think at the moment how to deal with that.' He bent to kiss her forehead, held her a moment more, then released her. 'The world is stirring. Will you try for some more sleep? Another hour will do you no harm.'

She was off balance, confused, needing time to think. 'An hour . . . an hour might be beneficial.'

'Sleep easy then. I shall not be far away.'

'Adam . . . '

He placed his fingertips on her lips. 'Later,' he said. 'My soul is too full. I do not want to do this wrong.' Then he ducked out of the barn, leaving Jenny alone with the whirlpool of her thoughts.

★ ★ ★

The Earl of Harwood. Adam remembered him from the bespoke at Radleigh Manor. His lip curled as he repeated the man's jest. *An African player? Do you have to beat his lines into him every night?* He grimaced, wishing he could wash the words out of his mouth. He had sounded just like the earl then. He'd always had a gift for mimicry. The ability to make people laugh had saved him from many a beating for not tallying his sums properly when he was young. Indeed, it was only in the last year or two that he'd stopped including parodies of public figures on the playbill. He preferred to act his own way now, to invest roles with his own reading of the character, not copy others who had played the parts before him.

Adam shifted irritably as he walked. The trouble was, when mimicking a man, he in some way became him. He'd only met the Earl of Harwood for a few minutes, barely mouthed his words, yet he felt sullied by the contact. He could understand Jenny escaping from him.

He thought of her, sleeping or wakeful, in the barn behind him. Her very name conjured a pool of easy calm into which he wanted to step; and yet she constantly wrong-footed him. He was used to summoning the best out of his company, he was accustomed to organising things and to dealing with people. Why could he not deal with Jenny?

She had not told him the whole truth when she'd first arrived, but she had explained that. She *had* done what she'd promised, diligently and honestly. She was quiet, not showy. She got on with what was needed and she was firm when she knew herself to be right. And when she'd said wretchedly that it would be best if she left, his body had reacted with a powerful denial. The shock from *that* was what had driven him outside. It reverberated within him still.

He paced the enclosure. He knew

what he wanted, of course he did. He was only a man, after all. It had been five months since Mary's passing; and even before that, though she'd always been willing, he'd frequently felt she was pressing physical affection on him for *him*, not for her.

He should be ashamed. Was he a monster to be thinking thus? Mary had sacrificed everything for him. She'd been the rudder in their relationship, steering their craft with a fierce and unswerving eye to where she had determined he wanted to go. Bad enough that he was considering changing the family's way of life in direct contradiction to her wishes, but at least that was only his head talking. This, behind him in the tent, was his heart.

Jenny had been in his arms. She'd felt so right there. She had felt like part of him in the way Mary never had. If she'd lifted her face to his a few moments ago, they would have kissed; and he had the growing suspicion that once he first kissed Jenny, he wouldn't stop his whole life long. He would have to resist the temptation. He could never bear the disillusionment in her eyes when she found out what he was. Besides, even less than Mary did Jenny belong in a company of strolling players.

He paced again, checking the barn was secure, checking that the wagons and horses were safely corralled. High-spirited bucks, with or without any losses on the day's racing, were all too apt to borrow a ride if any were easily offered. While he paced, he was considering what best to do, the safest course of action to take for the immediate future, and beyond. He was responsible. He had a duty to the well-being of his company, but he must also see to his own children and their lives. And now he must look after Jenny too. Before he let her go.

★ ★ ★

Jenny had rarely been abroad when one of the race meetings was on. The

210

theatre barn was on the outskirts of town, but there was enough of a crowd by the second day of their stay for her to understand why the Chartwell Players had not protested Adam's edict that the females of the company should keep within doors. The population of Newmarket must have swelled to six times its normal size — and all of them men.

It made it all the more surprising to hear a stranger's voice coming from the Jacksons' changing room while Adam was rehearsing the rest of the company on stage. She paused outside the door, irresolute.

'I must go,' she heard Lucy say. 'I should be on stage.'

'I would watch your performance again, but I daresay your manager will not welcome me here.'

Something Adam wouldn't like? Jenny pushed open the door. 'Lucy, I . . . Oh!'

It was clear Lucy and the young man had just sprung apart. 'Hello, Jenny.

211

Does Adam require me?' asked Lucy, recovering. 'Do you know Mr Browne, from the Norwich Company of Comedians? He was here to — '

'To compliment you on your acting, no doubt, and who could wonder at it? Do you watch us this evening, sir?'

'I . . . yes, if I may. I do not need to be in Bury St Edmunds until the end of the week.'

Jenny smiled at the flustered young man. 'Then you must certainly watch. I did not realise the Norwich Company would be at the Bury theatre next week. That seems earlier than usual, I think?'

'It would be, ma'am, if we were putting on a performance, but we do not play there until the Bury Fair. This is a matter of business only. Pray excuse me. It is delightful to make your acquaintance, but I must not interrupt the rehearsal further.'

Jenny followed Lucy thoughtfully to the main part of the barn. Later, when Adam was at leisure, she told him of the incident. 'Did you know this Mr

Browne was here? He is the actor who was mentioned at Cambridge, presumably? Do you know he is trying to fix his interest with Lucy? Her mother will have a number of words to say about that.'

'I noticed him slip through the door with her, yes. How could you doubt it when it is my theatre? But I did not consider him to be a hazard to the company at large.' His eyes crinkled in tolerant amusement. 'I have been considering which programme would show Lucy to best advantage.'

Jenny stared. 'You are serious, Adam? You would let your best actress go to the Norwich Company?'

His levity fell away. His face turned remote. 'I begin to think I would let them all go, provided I could manage affairs to their advantage. I do not want this life for Lottie.'

14

Jenny was extremely circumspect every time she had occasion to pass the open door of the barn, for fear of being recognised by former neighbours. Even so, she was not prepared for the extent of her shock at the dismaying sight of Cousin Vincent on a sleek black horse, stopping just outside, pointing towards the playboard where Billy and Chas were lounging and asking something of his companions. She fled to the narrow passage that Adam had fabricated behind the stage and found Samuel Obidah there, looking as grey and desperate as she herself felt inside.

For a moment they pressed their backs against the wall in a shared, shivering silence. 'This is no ague,' said Jenny once her throat had opened enough to allow her to speak. 'How long have you known the Earl of Harwood?'

The African's breathing came in harsh, laboured gusts. 'Centuries. I was his slave.'

Jenny stared. *Cousin Vincent's slave?* 'No, that's impossible. I have seen you acting with the Chartwell Players these two years.'

'It was before that. He lost me at cards one time when we were in England. I was there for show as his personal servant, standing behind his chair while he got drunker and drunker and dipped deeper into his pocket. I was thrown into the bet as a last act of bravado, to show what a great man he was, how rich, how careless of his possessions. My new owner, who had subtly goaded Mr Rooke into staking me, was an abolitionist. He made me a free man as soon as the game was ended.'

One time when we were in England? This was almost too much for Jenny to absorb in addition to the fright of seeing her cousin at all. 'One time when you were in England? You are telling me that the Earl of Harwood has visited this country before?'

'On many occasions. He is ruthless and ambitious. His business is three times what it was in his father's day. He has more plantations, more land, and he increases his fleet of ships every year. Jamaica wasn't big enough for him. He also has shipping interests in this country and he takes a fancy now and again to visit and see what he is the heir to. Liked the estate fine, the way he boasted when he came back the first time. I did not realise he had now inherited.'

'He never made himself known to us,' whispered Jenny, almost to herself. 'I had never seen him before he arrived last month. We thought him in Jamaica all these years. No wonder he has so large an acquaintance in this country already. I could not understand it before.'

Samuel turned his head. 'Your father was the previous earl? I'm sorry.'

His voice was compassionate, but

preoccupied. Jenny pushed aside her own conundrum and concentrated on him. 'If you are a free man, why do you still fear my cousin?'

He gave a grotesque smile. 'You know him and ask that? He does not lose lightly.' There was such a long pause Jenny thought he had finished. Then he sighed. 'I wake every morning amazed to be alive. I know too much.'

Yes, Cousin Vincent would not want his true character spread abroad in a country where he was desirous of establishing himself. A man who would shoot his own horse would feel no remorse over killing someone whom he probably still thought of as a slave. 'Then why come to Newmarket with the Chartwell Players?' she asked. 'It is madness. I should not be here myself except that I was out of my wits when we arrived.'

'Adam and Mary's original circuit was in the west country. I joined the Chartwell Players there because our ship docked at Bristol the time Mr

Rooke lost me at play. I had heard the name Rooke Hall in connection with the future earldom, but I did not know in which part of England it was. Mr Rooke always travelled alone when he came here. The Players had a run of bad luck and moved to East Anglia. I didn't think anything of it. Why would I? Hearing his voice at Radleigh Manor was my worst nightmare come to life. Are his wife and son with him in England?'

'His wife passed away on the voyage. Eddie is at Rooke Hall. He is a sweet-tempered child, but not strong.'

'And . . . and the child's nurse?'

There was a darker flush on Samuel's cheeks. Jenny smiled. 'My cousin brought his whole household. Ruth was well, the last time I saw her. I like her very much. But Samuel, Rooke Hall is only four miles up this road, near the village of Fordham. You must leave in the opposite direction as soon as possible. It is not safe for you here. An African player causes comment even if you are not acting on stage, as we heard at Radleigh. The presence of one amongst the Chartwell Players cannot fail to come to the Earl's ears. He would look for you simply out of curiosity. I can furnish you with money to get to London. If you go to my father's man of business, you can relate your history to him and sign it as a true record. It may not save your life if Cousin Vincent finds you again, but it will raise questions if anything happens to you.'

'Thank you. You do not ask what I know of the Earl?'

Jenny's attention became more focused. 'Have you evidence of something serious, then? More than just his everyday cruelty?'

Samuel gave a slow nod.

There was a quick footstep on the other side of the passage door. Adam burst through. 'Jenny?' Another two strides and he folded her to him. 'I saw the earl outside and thought . . . but you are safe. You are all right? He didn't spot you?'

His concern sent warmth coursing through her, telling her once again that this was now home, here in his arms. 'He didn't see me. But, Adam, it transpires Samuel is *not* safe. He knows something damaging about Cousin Vincent.'

Adam recollected himself. He let her go in some confusion and turned to the other man. 'Is this so? Then we had best go to the office and hear it.'

Samuel sat on a chair, leaning forward in order to keep the conversation quiet, gripping his thighs so hard Jenny fancied she could see old, faded scars circling his wrists.

'The earl trades in slaves,' he said, his voice barely above a breath.

Jenny felt her insides clench. 'No! That is illegal.'

The African's face was ghastly. 'This is why I am dangerous to him. I was his personal servant, so I know all his ways, all his secrets. His ships have two holds. The upper one is for sugar and molasses. The lower one is hidden, for human cargo. If naval cutters happen upon the ships in transit and signal a wish to board, the captains have orders to drown the slaves before they can talk.'

Jenny's hand went to her mouth. This was beyond everything.

'You know this for absolute fact?' said Adam intently, his eyes on Samuel's face. 'Enough to swear to it? It means transportation or hard labour for the earl if it's proven.'

'And hanging for murder,' said Samuel. 'I have seen it. I have heard Vincent Rooke give the orders with my own ears. I can swear to it in court.'

'Then of a certainty you must be on the next mail coach to Jenny's Mr Tweedie. And you must then go into hiding until he can get here with a Bow Street runner and a judge's warrant.'

Samuel bowed his head. 'I have tried to forget, tried to put it from my mind, treasured my own freedom to the detriment of my soul, but I knew this day would come,' he said. 'I should have told the man who freed me, but I was newly loose and too scared of Mr Rooke to do aught but get away. A lifetime's terror is not a simple thing to overcome.' He stood, looking drawn and old before his time. 'I quaffed my freedom in one draught and ran, but it has been much on my mind recently that it does not do to run forever.'

Adam gripped his shoulder, his face compassionate. 'One cannot always be strong alone. Strange as it may seem, I am glad you waited until now to face your past. I begin, dimly, to see a way forward.'

Jenny shivered. 'Do you? I should be perfectly happy to run for three months more, myself. *Then* I might consider stopping.'

Adam turned to her. 'And what when you have inherited?' he asked. 'What when you have willed your land and the river access away from your cousin? Do you truly think that will make you safe? Will the earl be content to have you living at your Prior's Ground, cheek by jowl with him, on land he considers should be his? Or will he seek to dispose of you anyway and then persuade your heir to sell to him when he has threat-ened them and set traps for them and made *their* life a living hell?'

Beyond him, Samuel nodded in sober agreement. Jenny stared at them both, her heart pounding. She had not thought one moment beyond her birthday. 'I do not know,' she whispered. 'Dear God, I do not know.'

Adam gave a small grim smile. 'It is as well one of us has been considering the road ahead. I may not be able to add up more than a single column of figures a fortnight, but I *can* plan. Today is Monday. Samuel, you leave tonight with a letter from Jenny, and I think . . . yes, I think you must persuade Mr Tweedie to take the stagecoach to Bury St Edmunds next week.'

'Bury?' said Jenny, startled. 'You told me the Norwich Company did not look kindly on rivals at any of their regular stops.'

'They don't, but I can turn that to good account. The main reason to go there is the circumstance of it being the nearest large town to here that Mr Tweedie can get to and easily find us. In addition, you will be out of the earl's way as far as accidental sightings are concerned. Finally, Bury St Edmunds is within reach of Rooke Hall, so if Mr Tweedie can obtain an arrest warrant, we can ride over and serve it on your cousin. It is also why I must needs write a new play.'

'A new play?' Had she heard him aright? Jenny was thoroughly bewildered. With all of this going on, Adam was thinking of writing a new play? Truly, men were the oddest creatures on this earth.

His eyes crinkled at her confusion. 'Did you never use a carrot to lead a donkey where he would not otherwise go? I said I could turn being in Bury to account. Travelling theatre troupes, even those as superior as the Norwich Company of Comedians, are always hungry for novelty. A new melodrama, well-advertised in advance, will stay their hand until they have conned it thoroughly enough to play it themselves. It will buy us time. Time enough, I trust, for Mr Tweedie to arrive.'

Jenny's thoughts whirled. He had thought of this plan so fast? For her? 'You are magnificent,' she said wonderingly.

He flushed. 'Jenny, I am not. Events are like loading a wagon; it is merely the fitting of things into place. Can you look through those stories you have been reading to Lottie and choose one that would make a good play? Not too long, for we do not have sufficient time to learn it. One that will make a useful opener or afterpiece.'

'I can,' said Jenny, and in truth she would be glad of the diversion. Her head was almost too full to think. The knowledge that Adam would arrange his schedule for her was a beguiling distraction, but there were also the grim revelations about her cousin to consider. If he could but be convicted! It was a dizzying thought. If sentenced, then he would be transported to the

Australian penal colonies, Eddie would become master of Rooke Hall, the steward would take care of the estate for him as he had always done, and she, Jenny, would be free to live at the Prior's House with Aunt Sophy.

Except . . . She glanced across the office to where Adam and Samuel had their heads together, talking in low murmurs. It was all very well sorting out *her* life, but what of Adam? He was not yet healed. He was certainly not happy. Even without the mesmerising thought that he was coming to care for her, how could she go back to her old life now and leave him here like this? A memory came to her. Adam, recalling Mary in her delirium crying out, '*What of him? Who will take care of him?*' Adam had assumed his wife to be grieving over her lost babe, but Jenny had Mary's measure now. She rather thought Mary had been anxious about Adam himself. And she seemed to have taken on that responsibility along with Mary Prettyman's ledgers.

* * *

That night, the takings were extraordinary. Adam stood at the entrance of the barn collecting the entrance fees, acting the good-humoured host with Joe Jackson to back him up, large enough to ensure all who came in knew no riotous behaviour would be tolerated.

Jenny sat out of sight in the office and counted the money. When she told Adam the total later, he stood quite still, his lips pursed in a silent whistle.

'This makes it conclusive that Billy Bidens was robbing us,' he said. 'It was much the same size audience earlier in the year and yet we did not take near so much.' His face turned as stern and remote as winter. 'He has been beggaring me while I have been giving him and his brother employment. As soon as we finish here, I will dispense with their services.' A certain dour humour crept into his smile. 'I shall tell them I can no longer afford them.'

15

Will, it transpired, had also been arriving at conclusions. He sidled into the office after Jenny had sent him to the baker next morning with a commission for penny buns, saying in an offhand voice that he had happened to meet a friend in the town whom he had brought back.

Jenny tilted her head to one side. 'Why are you telling me? People coming on to theatre land are surely your father's concern.'

Will looked even more guileless. 'I did think it might be your concern too,' he said as he opened the door and Rob Starling edged furtively through it.

Jenny's mouth fell open.

'I remembered the handbill,' explained Will, failing to look modest.

Pride in him washed through Jenny. 'You are extremely clever, and I will tell you the whole history later. For now, we will say if asked that your friend tore his shirt and you brought him to me to mend it so that he should not get into trouble at home.' She took a breath, organising her thoughts. 'Rob, pray tell your father that I am well and that we go next to Bury St Edmunds. What is the news of the Prior's Ground?'

The red-haired boy rubbed his nose. 'The earl is still saying as how he's acting for you, and he's started his men on drainage ditches. He's got a whole crowd of guests this week for the racing, so he's not over to Radleigh Manor courting so much, but the grooms think it's a done deal. Ma's taught the girls how to fight dirty but keeps them mostly within. Pa says we can stick it out.'

Jenny thanked him and sent them both off with thruppence for more treats. News, even so meagre, of home was like a knife twisting in her gut. They were her people, her responsibility, and she missed them with an intensity that made her heart ache.

229

More prosaically, being this close, she also dearly wished she could send to Penfold Lodge for extra small-clothes. Regretfully, any sudden addition to her laundry was the fastest way she knew to raise suspicions in the minds of the ladies of the company as to where it might have come from.

When Will returned quite a lot later with, ironically, a real tear in his own shirt, she told him and Lottie her story, but impressed upon them that they must not say anything to anyone in the company bar their father.

'I would like to see your house,' said Lottie wistfully. 'Is it as big as Susanna's?'

'Nothing is as big as Susanna's house,' said Jenny with feeling, having got lost daily on both occasions when she had visited Kydd Court with Caroline. 'Rooke Hall is quite large, but the Prior's House is very modest. Presently, however, it is extremely hazardous, for it is being repaired so I can live in it. The right-hand rooms are sound, but the ones on the left side of the house are so full of holes and planks and ladders that they resemble more a spider's web than a proper home.'

'Like a bird's nest,' said Will.

'Yes, a nest for a jenny wren,' laughed Lottie.

'I saw it this afternoon,' confided Will with sidelong look. 'Just the outside. I went back with Rob Starling to his farm. I saw your horse too. She's prime, isn't she?'

'Oh, Will, you did not,' said Jenny, alarmed. 'You did not go close enough to be remarked, I hope? But perhaps one boy looks much like another after all. I should enjoy showing you both over the Prior's Ground, but I dare not. My cousin will be watching continually for me or my agents. It would be by far too dangerous for any strangers to be seen anywhere on the estate. Three months is not so long to wait. Until then, I must keep safe and out of sight. It will be easier soon, for we will be on our way and clear of the Earl of Harwood's orbit. Now then, are you hungry?'

As always, the question was an excellent diversionary tactic. They emerged from the office, with Jenny well wrapped in an obscuring shawl, in search of Mrs Jackson and her stew pot. Ahead of them, Jenny saw Billy Bidens bent on the same errand.

'Are you cold?' asked Lottie, skipping beside her. 'I felt you shiver.'

Just someone walking over my grave, thought Jenny. 'A little,' she said aloud. 'It is a most unpleasant day. I pity the poor racehorses having to turn out in this. Do you think we shall ever have summer again?'

★   ★   ★

As Adam acted in the farce that night, a detached part of him studied the audience. Lucy's would-be swain was there again, a fact that had not escaped Mrs Jackson. Jenny's quiet remark about Mrs Jackson not letting her daughter go without a fight wove itself into his plans.

Of more concern was that the Earl of

Harwood was also present with a party of other men. All of them wore the hard-bitten look of merchants for whom ruthlessness was an accepted prerequisite for financial success. They drank from a decanter served by a dark-skinned servant crouching at his master's feet. The Earl showed no regard for the luckless man, at the mercy of the audience's trampling boots.

'Carriage,' he said in a cold voice at the end of the performance.

The servant hurried off. Adam disliked Jenny's cousin more and more.

'Tell me about the Earl,' he said into the darkness that night. He knew Jenny was still awake. Over the past weeks, he had learned to distinguish her quiet, even breathing when asleep, her distressed murmurs when dreaming, and her stillness when wakeful. Now he pictured her staring ahead into the darkness, and wanted to know where her thoughts were.

She sighed. 'I know very little about him. My grandfather's younger brother went out to Jamaica, where he bought a sugar plantation. Vincent is his grand-son. He is, I think, a man quite without soul. I grieve for my father's tenants. I fear for my cousin's son.'

'He has a child?' Adam didn't know why he should be so surprised. A man like that would naturally have ensured his succession before his wife's untimely — or timely — death.

'Yes, but the thought in the nursery is that he will not see maturity. Eddie takes after his late mother and is not strong. He is a nervous child, sweet-tempered when treated sensibly, but out-of-proportion scared of his father. That is not to be wondered at, for I have never seen the least hint of parental affection from the earl. My cousin married the only daughter of a neighbouring plantation owner. I understand from Eddie's nurse that it trebled his land. He does very little without reason.'

'What fortune does Miss Stavely have?'

'Sixty thousand pounds.'

Adam whistled. 'Then her days as a

single woman are surely limited.'

'I believe so indeed. And depending on the settlements, once she is brought to bed of a son, Eddie's days are likely also to be numbered. Miss Stavely is a powerful reason why my cousin would not wish to encumber himself with me.'

'I doubt many men would find you an encumbrance.' The words fell from his mouth naturally. He did not even hear them until they arranged themselves in the air.

There was the tiniest pause. 'It is kind of you to say so, but I cannot help feeling the presence of a murderous cousin at one's shoulder might take the shine off even the most ardent court-ship.'

Adam found himself giving a low chuckle. 'Jenny, you say the most absurd things. If we succeed and all the paths lead to the right places, it will hopefully be one less problem you have to contend with. Have you given thought to a suitable subject for a new play?'

'Demeter and Persephone,' said Jenny immediately. 'The story deals with the legend of the seasons, so will appeal throughout the countryside. Lucy will be joyous as Persephone, and Demeter is a gift for Mrs Jackson. You may write her a fine rousing speech for when she rails against Zeus for allowing her daughter to be given to Hades. If that does not show off her ability in front of the Norwich Company, nothing will.'

Adam lay perfectly still. 'Tell me, do you know what is in everyone's mind, or only in mine?'

Her voice came back with absolute conviction. 'Not everybody's by any means, but I begin to know you, Adam. You care. You care for *all* your people.'

At that moment, in the quiet darkness with only the gentle snores and soft shifting of sleeping bodies from the rest of the company to be heard outside the office walls, her soul seemed to touch his. It was as well, thought Adam wryly, that the children lay between them, preventing him from doing anything foolish.

He let out a carefully measured breath. Jenny was an earl's daughter and he was a strolling player. Time enough for a reckoning when all the threads were pulled tight.

'You had best refresh my memory,' he said. 'Demeter was a wife of Zeus, was she not?'

'They all were,' said Jenny drily. 'Zeus was a busy god.' Her voice fell into an age-old storytelling rhythm. 'Demeter was the goddess of the crops, as devoted to her beautiful daughter Persephone as Persephone was to her. Persephone was made for sunshine and warmth and laughter, but Zeus's brother Hades fell in love with her beauty and, with Zeus's consent, enticed her into his dark, cheerless underworld. When she heard what had happened, Demeter was overcome with fury and grief. She vowed she would let no more crops grow until she'd got her daughter back. Zeus, fearful of revolution by the starving people, sent Hermes to bargain with Hades for Persephone's return. Meanwhile, Hades had been wooing

Persephone with beautiful gifts and gentle words. She began to see the intelligent, tortured man beneath the god, but still she would not eat or drink for fear of never leaving his realm. Eventually, she fell enough in love with him to let him persuade her into eating just six juicy pomegranate seeds at the very moment that Hermes burst into the underworld to bring her back. This should have meant she had to stay, however Hermes bargained spiritedly with Hades and now Persephone spends six months below ground, when Demeter is sad and no crops grow, and six months above ground when Demeter is happy again and all is summer and harvest.'

The play unrolled in Adam's head as Jenny spoke. One act. Two at the most. With a humorous musical soliloquy for Mr Jackson as Zeus, on the subject of wives and daughters, and mirror-image dances by the young ladies depicting sunny harvest days above ground, wearing garlands in their hair, and then ghostly gloom in the underworld, with everyone in grey hoods to conceal the fact that they were doubling up on parts.

'Nothing could be more apt,' he said. 'Thank you. I will begin on it tomorrow. Then all we need do is charm the Norwich Company into letting us stay long enough in Bury St Edmunds that firstly, they get to watch us and like the play enough to bargain, and secondly, your Mr Tweedie arrives with a Bow Street Runner while we are still there to take your testimony and arrest your cousin the earl.'

And then, *then*, provided he could find the resolution in himself, he and Jenny must talk.

16

Billy and Chas Bidens were inclined to belligerence at being laid off.

'I regret the necessity,' said Adam heavily. 'Alas, finances are so very tight that I am hard pressed to pay back the company's accumulated debts as it is.'

Jenny did not at all like the look Billy bent on her as he and his brother took their final week's wages.

'Be easy,' murmured Adam. 'The rest of us will patrol the site until it is time to leave. I daresay the pair of them will follow the racing gentlemen back to London and try their luck in the variety theatres there.'

'I own I will feel more comfortable when there are sixty miles between us,' confessed Jenny. 'Where do we stay in Bury?'

'It will have to be somewhere with a large room or an inn yard. We'll not get a licence to set up in a barn. Do you know the town at all? In general we skirt around it, so I am not familiar with the different hostelries.'

'I know it very well. The Bushel near Risbygate would be best for our accommodation, but as for playing . . . ' Jenny moistened her lips. 'They do have a yard, but if you are wishful of attracting the attention of the Norwich Company of Comedians with as much speed as possible, you could perhaps apply to use the upper room in the Market Cross. It makes a fine auditorium and would bring in all the gentry in the area, for they are accustomed to going to plays there.'

Adam laughed. 'For sure, but the Norwich Company have the sole lease on that theatre. The corporation will never grant us even temporary use of the building.'

'Do you think so? Even if, as I believe to be the case, the corporation is presently experiencing a small difference of opinion with the Norwich

Company of Comedians? As I understand it, the manager is pressing for an expensive redecoration of the upper room, for which the corporation is not willing to bear the full cost. A temporary licence issued to another troupe could be seen as a warning shot across the bows, perhaps?'

Adam stared at her, amazed. 'Jenny, how do you know this?'

'I am close friends with Alderman Taylor's daughter, Louisa, who is Caroline Rothwell's great friend and sister-in-law. Her father tells Louisa everything, and she tells the rest of the world. I do not think there would be much difficulty obtaining a licence. I told you I took them both under my wing at school. Absurdly, Alderman Taylor still feels he owes me an obligation. Additionally, it is Louisa's birthday next week, and the alderman dearly loves a play.'

'So if nothing else, we might do a bespoke? You would come with me to apply for the licence?'

'Of course. He will think it very odd of me, no doubt, but he will not give me away. Or we could present you as a friend of Susanna and Kit, perhaps. That might serve better. When do you think to travel? He has a goldsmith's shop in the town, so keeps early hours. We should still lodge at the Bushel. Even more than Haverhill, Bury is a respectable town.'

'I agree. Playing at the Market Cross . . . we will not know ourselves. I had best set to and finish writing the play.' He paused, his hand going out to touch her arm, his expression softening into more than warmth. 'Thank you, Jenny. It was a very fortunate day for me when you walked into the barn in Clare.'

Jenny's heart pulsed. *For me too, Adam. For me too.*

⋆　⋆　⋆

It was fifteen weary miles through more rain and mud before the company was at last ensconced in the Bushel Inn at

Bury St Edmunds. It was too late to pay any calls that day, but Alderman Taylor was in transports to see Jenny the next morning, and he readily granted the Chartwell Players a licence to play in the town.

'The Market Cross, eh?' He tapped his teeth, thoughts chasing themselves across his face. 'Yes, yes I believe it will serve very well. You will not mind if I dash off a note to the Norwich Company of Comedians letting them know they may not have the playhouse next week?'

Adam assured him with a straight face that he would not mind in the least and asked if he had a favourite play for the day of his daughter's birthday. 'For we are putting on a new piece several times during the week, but as you have been so very obliging, I would be happy to oblige in turn by leaving one of the other choices on the programme to you.'

The alderman turned pink with pleasure. 'Oh, anything amusing, you know. Say, what is that one where the steward is made out to be in love with the lady? That's a capital play, is that.'

'I think you mean *Twelfth Night*, do you not?' said Jenny. 'The one that opens with a shipwreck?'

'And the girl dressing as the boy and all in love with the wrong person. Yes, that's the one. Well, well, *Twelfth Night* then, and your new play and a few rousing songs all for the Thursday. Splendid. Louisa will be delighted. Will you dine with us beforehand, my dear?'

Jenny's heart gave a startled thump. She had become so accustomed to thinking herself one of Adam's company that she had entirely forgotten the day-to-day doings of her former life. 'I think I must decline, sadly. It is most kind of you to invite me, and nothing would normally give me greater pleasure, but I am keeping as far as possible out of public life until my majority is reached. My cousin has very little love for me on account of the Prior's Ground.'

'Oh, aye, yes. Caroline mentioned as

much. Bad business. The earl will not be present, of course.'

'He may well know some among your guests, however, who might remark that they met me at your table. At present he is unsure of my whereabouts. I prefer to keep myself from his notice. It has been lovely to see you again, Alderman, but we should not intrude any longer on your business hours. Mr Prettyman has the plays to rehearse.' She was aware that there was nothing Louisa's father would have liked to do more than chat to them all morning, but she was concerned to get away before he could ask where, in fact, she *was* staying. Mr Tweedie might have contented himself with describing her present arrangements as unconventional, but if the Alderman knew she was at the Bushel, he could easily take it upon himself to call. Once he realised she was sharing a room with Adam and his children, no matter that Will and Lottie were extraordinarily effective chaperones, her reputation would be in tatters.

'Another time then,' he said now. 'Mr Prettyman, you'll step back this afternoon to sign the agreement and collect the keys? My clerk will have done all the necessary by then.' He paused, a contemplative look on his face. 'Prettyman,' he murmured. 'I've come across the name before. Customer, I daresay. Suffolk family?'

Adam smiled pleasantly. 'I'm afraid not. Staffordshire.'

'Ah well.' He gave them his hand to shake and they took their leave.

★ ★ ★

When Jenny had first joined the company, Adam had said he had no family. It struck her now that this could not always have been the case. Did his origins, she wondered, go any way towards explaining the man he was now? She was just framing a casual enquiry about the Staffordshire countryside when she saw a most unwelcome sight.

'It is the Bidens brothers, coming

straight up the street towards us,' she cried, turning back as though to look in the goldsmith's shop window. 'Why would they be here? You thought they would head for London.'

Adam was as taken aback as she. 'I assumed they would. It makes no sense to follow us unless they also think to apply to the Norwich Company. They'll not succeed if so.'

The discharged actors had unpleasant smirks on their faces. 'Well now, brother,' said Billy to Chas as they came level. 'See who it is. No money for our wages, but enough for a licence to play the snuggest little market town in Suffolk.'

'It sometimes happens that a judicious sum laid out will see a useful return,' replied Adam neutrally. 'Good day, gentlemen.'

'That goes for buying a geegaw for your ladybird too, does it?' Billy's gaze wandered in an offensive manner from the trinkets in the window to Jenny, taking in her pretty bonnet and best gown.

Jenny pulled her cloak tighter, wishing it had not been necessary to dress as modishly as she could manage for visiting Alderman Taylor.

Adam flexed his hands absently. 'I do not believe that is any of your concern,' he said. 'Pray do not let us detain you. I have a play to rehearse.'

'I look forward to watching it,' called back Billy with a loud laugh.

'I do not trust them,' said Jenny worriedly once they were out of earshot.

'Nor I. I had best invest an extra sum with the innkeeper to keep our wagons protected. Fortunately, this town enjoys a good play, so if they think to disrupt our bill of entertainment by way of revenge, they will get short shrift from the audience.'

★ ★ ★

Sunday presented a problem to Jenny. The Chartwell Players always went to church when they could, in order to earn the goodwill of the town. Today they proposed strolling back via the Market Cross in order to become accustomed to the building. Jenny might have managed the church service by staying near the back, but she had too many acquaintances here to take a Sunday promenade unremarked.

Under the pretence of a slight cold and the inclement weather, she regretfully said she thought it would not be advisable to accompany them and that she would be better employed remaining in the inn parlour and continuing to make copies of the new play. She was surprised to be visited by Lucy Jackson before they left, ostensibly to bring her a phial of lavender water to dab on her temples and as a by-the-by asking if she might borrow Jenny's bonnet.

'For it is so charming that if Mama were to see me wearing it, she might advance me a sum to purchase a new one for myself.'

Jenny made a sympathetic response and granted the request. If the bonnet attracted the attention of Mr Browne, which she judged to be the purpose of the loan, then it would have done a good day's work.

She made excellent progress with copying the play, but it was surprisingly dull to be by herself like this. She realised with no little surprise that she had become accustomed to living in close quarters with the Chartwell Players. It now seemed very quiet without the noise and bustle as they all went about their daily business. She stood gladly when an uproar from downstairs announced their return. They burst into the parlour talking volubly, Lucy and her mother being the loudest. Lucy, it seemed, had nearly been robbed while crossing one of the alleys on the way back from the theatre.

'It had stopped raining,' she said, fanning herself vigorously. 'So Adam put down his umbrella and I fell back a little from the others as I had a stone in my shoe. Then an arm shot out from around a corner and grabbed me! As soon as I screamed, Adam and Joe gave chase, but the man ran away faster than them down the alley and we lost sight of him.'

'What a dreadful thing to happen in such a respectable town,' said Jenny, shocked. 'I shouldn't wonder if you didn't have an excellent turnout to watch you on Tuesday. It will be the townsfolk's way of showing sympathy.'

'Every cloud has a silver lining,' pronounced Mrs Jackson.

'I have finished another copy of Demeter and Persephone,' said Jenny, handing her the pages. 'Another hour will see the last one done.'

Lucy fixed her mother with a speculative eye. 'About Persephone's dress . . . ' she began.

'Rehearse first, Missy. Sew later.'

'Or we could sew *as* we rehearse,' said Lucy, pursuing her mother out of the door. 'We have the amber silk we bought at Midsummer Fair.'

'Was she really attacked?' Jenny asked Adam in a low voice. 'It wasn't Mr

Browne trying for a misguided assignation?'

'That was my first thought, but she was genuinely alarmed,' returned Adam. 'The man was too heavy-set for Mr Browne. Not that any of us saw his face, just a muffler and the back of his coat as he fled.'

'It was exciting,' averred Lottie, balancing on one foot and trying for a pirouette. 'You should have been there. Is your cold better? Did you miss us?'

Jenny swept her up for a kiss. 'I did. It was quiet and peaceful and I did not get on with it at all.'

Lottie wriggled down. 'You need us and we need you,' she sang, sounding as if she was adapting one of this morning's hymns.

Jenny's eyes met Adam's over Lottie's head. She was beginning to think Lottie was right, but Adam's guarded expression gave no indication as to whether the feeling was mutual. What a puzzle the man was. The other morning she could have sworn she meant more to

253

him than simply being the company assistant.

Sunday flowed far more easily now, and on Monday, they loaded one of the wagons and went early to the theatre. 'It is a new challenge, this living in one place and putting on our plays in another,' said Adam cheerfully, selecting boxes and trunks. 'I feel as stimulated as when Mary first persuaded me that after being abandoned by our manager, we should start our own company of players — and I suddenly found myself planning for a dozen people rather than just ourselves.'

Jenny shook her head in admiration as she watched. He was in his element, deciding what needed to go with them and what could stay and where to pack it all in. 'Where does this knowledge come from?' she marvelled. 'Were your ancestors master carters that you always know just where things should be placed for best effect?'

He glanced at her in amusement. 'My

ancestors would be rising from the crypt in outrage if you even suggested such a thing. I do not know, Jenny. I was born with it. It is nothing out of the ordinary, after all.'

Now that is where you are wrong, thought Jenny. *You are far from ordinary, Adam Prettyman.*

The rest of the day was a blur of rehearsing and scene setting, hasty advertisement delivering, and at last all was set for an opening bill of *Hamlet,* followed by *Wives as they Were and Maids as they Are.*

'Cut price for the short notice,' said Adam. 'Word will spread and we will get a better house for the new play tomorrow. Will you take the money? I will stand downstairs with you.'

'Yes, a close bonnet and drab cloak will suffice,' said Jenny. 'No one will be expecting to see me, so I should be safe from discovery.'

That night at the inn, lying in the bed by the window with Lottie while Adam shared the other with Will, she thought again of what had been running through her head all day. She had grown used to the Chartwell Players. It was difficult to imagine not being with them. She did, most desperately, want to get her cousin convicted and sent overseas, well away from Rooke Hall; but when he was, she would be free to go home. And quite apart from the continuing puzzle that was Adam, how was she herself to manage then? How was she to live comfortably alone once this travelling, laughing, busy life was no longer hers?

17

Demeter and Persephone, or *A Seasonal Story* was received very well on its first outing on Tuesday night. Adam had already decided to rest it on the Wednesday, rehearsing it again, ready to put it on once more on Thursday along with the alderman's *Twelfth Night.*

'Today is market day, so we'll all get abroad with handbills this morning,' he said at breakfast on Wednesday. The company nodded, thinking he was drumming up custom and thoroughly approving the likely increase in their wages for the week. Only Jenny knew he was determined to get word to the Norwich Company by any means he could.

'Take Will and Lottie with you to the livestock market,' she suggested to him. 'Farmers come in from all around the area, so you should find ready custom and the news will then spread. Meanwhile, I will see what flowers are to be found from the general market for headdresses for the Summer Maidens dance.'

'I would prefer it if you came with us,' said Adam with a frown.

'It would be commented on. Livestock auctions are for men and children only.'

Still he looked troubled. 'Take care then. We are not far off an end now.'

'I hope so. I did impress on Mr Tweedie in my letter that we could not reasonably stay in the town beyond a week. With luck, he is even now on his way with a warrant, then all will be resolved and I will no longer be a bother to you.' And as he still frowned, she continued, 'You may be easy, Adam. I will go out only to buy the flowers and put them in water ready to weave tomorrow.'

Which she did. The greenroom smelt heavenly. It would be a shame to lose their bounty when she fashioned them into headdresses. Maybe she should get more? There was also, Jenny reflected belatedly, as her stomach gave a healthy grumble, the question of food. It was all very fine sending Will off with Adam, but it meant she had no messenger to supply her with pasties or pies for a nuncheon.

She glanced out of the window. The town was more crowded now, but she should still be safe from discovery. She slipped on her bonnet and cloak and stepped out. She had gone perhaps a dozen paces before the world went black.

★   ★   ★

'Where is Jenny?' asked Lottie, dancing ahead of Adam into the greenroom.

Adam looked around. Jenny had evidently been here, judging by the presence of the flowers, but there was no sign of her in the room otherwise. 'I don't know, sweetheart. Go and have a look. We must get on with the rehearsal.'

But they had only just embarked on the first of tonight's plays when Lottie was back. 'She's not in the office, Papa, and not in the dressing rooms.'

'Perhaps she had to go back to the inn for something. Come and do your scene now.'

But the afternoon wore on, and Jenny still did not appear. Snaking tendrils of anxiety crawled through Adam. If she was concerned about being recognised, he could understand her remaining at the inn, but what if she was ill and they did not know it? He sent Will and Lottie back to the Bushel to see if aught was amiss. They returned in a rush, eyes wide, tear streaks on Lottie's face, in such a fever of anxiety that the blood ran cold in Adam's veins.

'There was a note,' said Will, breathing hard and gulping down his worry. 'It had only just been delivered. A messenger handed over the note and left straight away. The potboy couldn't say what the messenger looked like.'

Adam opened the letter, already

knowing that it would not be all right. He was aware of Lottie and Will watching him anxiously and the rest of the company drawing closer.

'It is in her hand,' he said. The words blurred and he blinked to clear them.

'That's not her paper,' said Lottie. 'And all her things were still there. Nothing has been moved since this morning.'

My dear Adam . . .

So formal. She had gone away. Left them. She had said as much earlier. Why had he not cried out then that she was not a bother, that she would never be a trouble to him? Why had he put off the conversation they should have had by now? Must he always be so weak? Oh, how could he bear this?

'Papa,' said Lottie, shaking his arm.

He started again, reading aloud to keep his thoughts steady.

My dear Adam,
Pray excuse the shortness of the notice, but I am writing to let you

know that whilst marketing this morning, I met a friend who has invited me to her husband's country estate for a few weeks to relieve her boredom and solitude. She was travelling at that very hour and could not wait, so might I trouble you to pack up my boxes, please, and I will send a carrier for them. Tell Lottie and Will that by all accounts there are birds' nests and spiders' webs aplenty there, so I shall not be neglecting our nature studies.

With thanks for your hospitality and all good wishes for the remainder of your tour,
Yours,
Jenny

'That's a poor sort of letter,' remarked Mrs Jackson disapprovingly. 'I'm surprised at her.'

'It is not real,' said Lottie, squirming to see the page.

Adam made himself answer. 'Sweetheart, it is in her own hand.'

'But there is no wren to say she is safe. She always puts one on. She told us, didn't she, Will? Once when she was a little girl and unhappy, she left it off and her papa came to fetch her away. She means us to go and get her.'

Adam's heart, which had sunk lower than the soles of his boots, struggled back up a little. 'How? How are we ever to find her direction? She has been gone for hours.'

'I know where she is,' said Will slowly. 'Read it again, Pa.'

'You cannot know. There is no address. She says she will send a carrier.'

'Read it, Pa,' insisted Will. 'Read the bit about the spiders.'

Adam turned back to the page. It made no sense. The words swam before his eyes. *My dear Adam* . . . If he had been in any doubt about the strength of his feelings, he knew them for real now.

Lottie took the letter from him, tracing the words as she read them out. *'Tell Lottie and Will that by all accounts there are birds' nests and spiders' webs a-plenty there* . . . Oh!' She smiled widely and met her brother's eyes, her own shining. 'Oh, yes, I see! She is at the Prior's Ground. That is how she described the rooms in her house. It is being mended so she can live there. That's clever. Is it a game?'

Will was shaking his head stubbornly. 'Not a game, for there is no wren on the page. She has told us where she is and she has told us to come and get her. Has she been taken there, Pa? Is she being kept there by her cousin?'

Adam stared at his children. Their absolute certainty convinced him. And after all, what could be more likely? It was market day. People travelled into the town from the surrounding area. The earl had presumably come across her unexpectedly whilst she was out and had snatched her up there and then.

The earl. The man who wants her land.

Rage filled him. Rage and fear. It was a moment before he could channel it into a useful direction.

'Her cousin?' said Mrs Jackson. 'What's all this?'

Adam answered, his mind lurching into life to consider possible actions. 'Jenny is not of Mary's family; she is a friend of Susanna and is, I think, in mortal peril. She hid with us for safety but has evidently been discovered.' He glanced at the clock. 'There is no time to rescue her now; we must play very soon. The mere fact of the note tells us she still lives and has her wits about her. Will, I must take one of our horses to Newmarket tonight. Can you saddle the best for me as soon as we get the wagon back to the inn? Fortunately, the moon is on the wax, so there will be a little light to see by.' Astoundingly, from being desperate, his spirits had lifted as if they were bounding up a mountain.

'The innkeeper has a riding horse,' said Will, and in the same breath, 'I'm coming too. I have been to her house. I went with Rob Starling. I can show you where to go.'

'And me,' said Lottie. 'You mustn't leave me behind. I will be good as good. I love my Jenny.'

'Lottie, you cannot come. I know you are fond of Jenny, but this might be dangerous. And . . . and there will not be room on the horse.'

'There will, Pa. It is a good animal. Jenny's own horse is at the Starling farm for the way back,' said Will. 'We can go there first. Lottie can wait with Rob's ma.'

Adam looked at them, his mind racing ahead, playing out increasingly desperate scenarios. In one set of circumstances, it would be imperative to have the family all together, but he was hoping it wouldn't come to that.

Mr Jackson cleared his throat. 'You'll not shift their minds,' he said. 'It'll ease yours having them with you, knowing where they are. Send young Will now for the innkeeper's hack, and then slip away after the first curtain. We'll close up and take the wagon back.'

The others nodded agreement.

'Thank you,' said Adam, accepting the inevitable, grateful beyond measure for his troupe's support.

★   ★   ★

Jenny paced her chamber in the Prior's House, more furious than she had ever been in her life. From the moment that disgusting sack had been pulled over her head by Chas Bidens and she'd been bound, bounced and jolted here in a cart, to when the sacking hood was pulled off and she'd faced her cousin, here on her own land, she had been blazing with rage.

At least she was alone in her room now, even if the vile Bidens brothers were roaming the rest of her house, keeping watch on all the doors in case she contrived another escape. She looked with satisfaction at the chest she had pulled across the door. The earl may have forbidden them to touch her until he returned tomorrow, but she placed no such trust in their honour, not after the way their hands had been *everywhere* as they carried her out of the cart and into the house.

'A lesson,' had said Vincent, Earl of Harwood, sitting at his ease in *her* best chair in *her* parlour. 'It is unwise to cross people, however insignificant they appear to be to you. Your erstwhile colleagues couldn't tell me where you were fast enough after you caused their dismissal.'

Jenny had inclined her head, enunciating carefully whilst ridding her mouth of dust from the sack. 'My thanks, cousin, but a written discourse on the subject would have sufficed. It did not need the physical reinforcement. I assume, now I have absorbed your tenet, you will let me go.'

The earl's eyes were cold, reminding her with a jolt that he had no sense of humour. She had forgotten the sheer joylessness of his rule whilst she'd been living with the Chartwell Players. 'You assume wrong,' he said. 'Opponents only ever lead me one dance, and you have already been tiresome beyond patience. You will remain here until you sign certain papers that I will have drawn up.'

'Kidnapping is illegal.'

He ran his whip in a measured fashion through his fingers. 'I fail to see how it can be kidnap when you are in your own house on your own property. On which point, incidentally, I believe the most sensible course of action may be to restrict your movements for your own safety. Parts of this house seem sadly unsafe, so your companions here have orders to keep you under very close observation. Such a shame if you were to break your neck tumbling down the stairs due to an incautious step.'

Jenny did not look behind her at her abductors. 'Companions? My gaolers, you mean. Are they your men now? You may need to question their interpretation of loyalty. As well as feeling my person with a most unnecessary thoroughness, Billy stole my mother's ring from off my finger as he tied my wrists. Was that on your orders? I should like it back, if you please. It came to me through her family, not the Rookes, and has sentimental value.'

'Untie her and return the ring.' The earl's voice lashed out as fast as his whip cracked past her. 'Traceable items are tickets to the docks if they are found on your person. You should be grateful to me.'

There was an oath from behind Jenny and a vicious punch in her back as her arms were untied.

'My ring?'

It was slapped into her open hand.

Jenny continued to address her cousin as she pushed the ring back on her finger and then rubbed her wrists. 'Thank you. You do realise that my friends will come after me? I'd back Mr Prettyman against Billy any day, even with his brother to hold an opponent down.'

'But you would not give such long odds on the children, I think?' replied her cousin dispassionately. 'Especially the little girl, in that ludicrously insecure tavern. Such a sweet appear-ance of innocence, but who knows what weapons she might be concealing that my men would have to probe for.'

His pale, inhuman eyes held Jenny's for a long moment. Cold struck at her heart. She stared back in horror.

'Precisely,' he continued. 'I am glad we understand each other. This is why you are going to write your former hosts a charming note explaining your absence to put their minds at rest. They will get it today, no alarms will be raised, and no harm will come to anyone.' He stood in a fluid movement and forced her into the chair, his hand biting into her shoulder. 'No tricks, please. I am watching every word. No formal language in the letter, for example, when I am informed you have been living on terms of intimacy with these vagabonds for several weeks.'

Jenny glanced at Billy. 'What a life,' she remarked. 'Listening at doors. Poking through personal belongings. I do hope you have been paid well for your information. It will be some small consolation to you when Adam rends you limb from limb.'

Billy made to cuff her back-handed, but was brought up by a snarl and another snap of the whip from the earl. 'Keep to your place,' he said. 'You have had your fun. This one is now mine, and I do not intend to have her marked beforehand.' His fingers dug further into her shoulder.

Jenny bent her head. Baiting the Bidens brothers and driving tiny wedges between them and her cousin was all very well, but she needed to *think*. How was she to convey where she was in her letter without the earl detecting her clues? That Adam would take action as soon as he was aware of her location, she was in no doubt whatsoever.

Her shoulder received another hard twist. 'Write,' repeated Cousin Vincent, a dangerous edge to his voice. 'And in case you are thinking of shouting for help, we are quite alone here. I laid off your workmen as soon as you vanished from Penfold Lodge. You are at my — and these gentlemen's — mercy.'

Workmen. Of course. Jenny let out a silent breath. *Thank you, cousin.* She dipped her pen, confident now that she had the right words. *My dear Adam . . .*

18

The innkeeper's horse was a surprisingly good one, and it was not yet quite dark, making the ride to Newmarket speedier than it might otherwise have been.

'He got him in exchange for an unpaid tab,' explained Will in answer to Adam's comment. 'Keep going past our theatre-barn for a while. Then there's a tidy lane on the right that leads to Rob's farm. From there we can cut across the fields. Rob said his pa has the key to the side door.'

'Let us hope the hinge does not squeak. Tell me again which rooms to avoid?'

Lottie spoke in a muffled voice from her place squashed between him and her brother. 'The back stairs are rotten and the floorboards on the left of the house are unsafe. The front stairs and the rooms to the right are sound, Jenny says. I want her back, Papa.'

Adam dropped a kiss on the top of his daughter's head. 'So do I, sweetheart.' *I just have to find the courage to tell her. And then tell her why I am no good for her.*

The Starlings had retired for the night, but were roused by Will swarming up on to the outhouse roof and in through Rob's window.

'Thought something was afoot,' rumbled Farmer Starling, lighting the kitchen lantern. 'The earl's got guests up at the Hall, but I seen a couple of flash roughs hanging about the Prior's House today. When I challenged them, they said to clear off and they were safeguarding the property on the earl's orders. I'll be glad to give you a hand with that pair, Mr Prettyman.'

Adam nodded. 'Thank you, but if we can do it without you being recognised, it would be preferable. I won't have him calling down the law on you if it can be avoided. See to the horses, Will, and look after Lottie. As soon as I've got Jenny safe, I want to be away as if we were never here.'

Keeping to the hedges, Farmer Starling led him quietly to the Prior's House. 'You've no doubt of rescuing Miss Jenny, then?' he said in a curious voice.

'None,' replied Adam. There was very little light in the lane, but his eyes were accustomed to the shadows and his tread was sure. 'If her guards are asleep, we take them by surprise in their slumber. If they are awake, I'll draw them out.'

'And if the Earl is there?'

Adam smiled grimly in the darkness. 'Life is rarely that obliging.'

★   ★   ★

There was nothing in Jenny's chamber apart from the furniture she'd had moved her during the days following her father's death. Cousin Vincent had inspected it earlier, treated her request

276

for a candle with the derision it deserved, locked her in and taken the key away with him. It seemed the earl was not giving her the chance to escape from him a second time. As soon as she had watched him depart, she had rested on the mattress for an hour. Now she paced slowly back and forth in front of her window in the hopes that her pale shawl and moving silhouette would be seen from outside.

Jenny's mind was studded with calculations. Fifteen miles from Bury. Say two hours with a good riding horse, but more likely three. Adam would not have got her letter in anywhere near sufficient time to leave during the afternoon, so he would have to play at least the first half of tonight's bill, possibly all of it. That put his likely arrival any time between eleven pm and three in the morning. She would be ready, but surely there must be some action she could take on her own account in the meantime? She appraised her resources, assessing with disfavour the merits of stout wooden drawers and padded footstools as either weapons or tools of escape.

She was aware that Adam would look at this room and no doubt flex his fingers in glee at its bounty. She, however, had neither the knowledge to take apart chairs for use as cudgels, nor the strength to prise out the nails which prevented her windows from being opened. Why had Papa never seen fit to include a study of carpentry in her education? She was all words, and mending linen, and balancing figures.

No . . . not quite all. She also had logic.

Then use it, Jenny.

What were her most pressing objectives? To get out of the room. To incapacitate the Bidens brothers. To escape.

How could she achieve all this? A key to the door or a lever for the window. Rope to tie up Billy and Chas . . . and for them to stand handily still whilst she did so.

What did she have? Her wits and the

clothes she stood up in.

She crossed to the wall. She also had her memory. There was a cupboard behind the panelling in this room, invisible to the naked eye. She hadn't dared open it yet in case it screeched and gave her away. Now though, she could hear Billy and Chas arguing downstairs. She waited until they were in full flow, then inserted her little finger into the knothole in the panelling and eased the section open. There was the quietest rub of wood against wood, then a dark space appeared in front of her. At first glance in the dimness, the shelves looked bare, apart from the pale glimmer of a basin and ewer. But at the side of the top shelf, her questing hand felt the comforting shapes of a candle and tinderbox should she need them. And at the very back of the next shelf down . . . yes . . . praise be, her spare ring of keys, left here for the workmen. *Thank you, my very prescient former self.*

Now, what to do with them. It would

be of no use to let herself out of this room when she would have to go downstairs past the Bidens brothers. From what she'd made out of the argument, they'd been throwing dice as to which of them kept watch whilst the other slept or went for food. Unfortunately, her cousin's whip had instilled enough respect that at least one of them was bound to be guarding the hallway.

The problem was, even if she lured Billy or Chas in here — or better still, into the room across the passage with the jagged hole in the floorboards — she could not tie them up without rope of some description. Luring them would be so easy to do, too. All it would take would be a mysterious noise.

Jenny sighed. It was a shame she had left her workbag in the theatre. She could have finished knitting Will's new stockings while she sat here waiting for Adam and planning what to do as soon as she heard him. Oh, wait! Knitting . . . Rope . . .

With a regretful sigh, she removed

the shawl from her shoulders and felt carefully around the edge.

★　★　★

There was only one room showing a light as Adam and Farmer Starling crept closer to the house. The ground floor at the front. It seemed highly improbable that Jenny would be any-where with such easy access. That must be where the guards were.

'Across here behind the stable,' whispered the farmer. 'The side door leads into the kitchens.'

Adam nodded. 'We don't know how many men he's got there now,' he said, 'but they are unlikely to be very sharp if they're working for him. I'm going to mimic his voice and draw them out one by one. Stand by with that cudgel of yours.'

He hefted the key in his hand, feeling the satisfying weight of the metal, the familiar shape of keys the country over. His head was cool, his temper steady. A long time ago he had gone into a fight, hot with righteous anger — and had very nearly paid the price for it. It had led indirectly to the life he was living now. His fury at Jenny's capture today was even greater than the rage he'd felt then, but he'd learnt over the years to compress anger into a channel of energy that he could tap to propel his fists or pump his legs as the occasion demanded. He turned the key in the door, opened it with a soft click, and found himself in the servants' passageway at the back of the house.

Farmer Starling pointed silently towards a door at the far end. Adam nodded. Easing it open gently, he put his eye to the crack. On the other side of the door, the walls were panelled, and a graceful staircase ascended into the shadows above. A candle flickered on the hall table. There were snores coming from the lit room at the end, but crucially a man was sitting in a hard chair with his back to them, watching the stairs and the main door.

Adam leaned against the wall of the kitchen passage, forcing himself to stay calm. He knew every one of his company and he knew now that Chas Bidens was in the hall of Jenny's house and those were Billy's snores. Furthermore, he realised it had been Chas's back he'd seen making off down the alleyway when Lucy Jackson had been attacked. They must have been after Jenny, even then and had grabbed Lucy by mistake.

Adam's hatred for the brothers swelled until he could barely contain it inside his skin. Scum. Whale bait. They had been robbing him all these months and now, in revenge for having their supply of ready funds cut off, had presumably kidnapped Jenny and sold her to the earl for a reward. *That* was why they had followed the company to Bury. It made sense. It was far more likely that *they* had watched and waited for a moment when Jenny was alone than that her cousin had just happened to see her unexpectedly. They must have overheard him and Jenny talking, or perhaps had found something amongst Jenny's belongings indicating her connection with Rooke Hall. This altered the situation dramatically. Had Jenny's gaolers been the earl's servants, he must and would have taken care how he incapacitated them. As it was, her rescue was going to be simpler, and more enjoyable, than he'd expected.

He thought swiftly. The Bidens brothers plainly hadn't received any reward money from the earl yet, since they were still here. Adam planned to ensure they never would. He leaned towards the farmer. 'Two men,' he murmured in his ear. 'I know them both. Stay out of sight, but if it's necessary, there's no need to worry how hard you hit them.'

It was hardly the pugilistic code, but the days when Adam had politely fought by the rules were long gone. He crept up behind Chas and pulled the back legs of the chair sharply from under him, causing the man to land flat on his face. Throwing the chair aside,

Adam thumped his knees down on to his adversary's back, driving all the wind out of his lungs. He ignored Chas's gasps for breath, twisted his arms behind him, and tied them with a loop of twine.

Impersonal and efficient, the manoeuvre had taken less than three minutes. Enough, however, to wake his brother up. Billy staggered into the hall, took one look at the tangle of body and chair, another at Adam, rising like the day of judgement to his feet, and raced upstairs with an oath, snatching a knife from his belt as he went.

Jenny! But even as Adam formulated the thought, he heard a shockingly loud scrawp as of a window casement being forced upwards.

'Jenny,' he yelled, taking the stairs two at a time in Billy's wake. Dear heaven, she mustn't try to escape by the window. How could she be that desperate? He faltered at the sound of a crash and a wild yell of pain, then powered on. Was she hurt? A red miasma of rage filled him as he burst through a half-open door on one side of the passage.

'Stop,' called Jenny urgently. 'Stay right there.'

Adam caught at the doorframe to halt himself, so glad to see her silhouetted safely by the far window that he didn't at first take in the scene in the middle of the room. It wasn't until Jenny skirted very carefully around the edges of the walls to get to him that he realised a large part of the floor was missing. Billy Bidens was stuck fast in a litter of jagged floorboards right in the very centre.

'You bloody witch,' yelled Billy. 'Get me out. I think I've broken my leg.'

Jenny cast the man a disparaging glance. 'I must remember to send you my carpenter's account for the extra work,' she said in the coolest voice Adam had ever heard from her, and drew him out through the door.

In the passageway, he wrapped his arms around her and held her as if he would never let her go. 'Are you safe?' he asked. 'Unharmed? God help me, I'll kill them both.'

'There is no need. I am bruised and angry as fire, but otherwise I'm well enough. Oh, Adam, I'm so enormously pleased to see you.'

'I came as soon as I could.'

She hugged him tighter. 'I knew you would be on your way. I had my hidden key and was waiting for any sound at all from downstairs. I knew I could trap at least one of that precious pair in the broken floorboards, because they'd be so intent on stopping me escaping that they'd take the hole in the floor for shadows.'

'You are everything that is wonderful. Chas is tied up in the hall. Come, let's get away.'

Downstairs, they collected Farmer Starling and left as quietly as they'd arrived. 'The Bidens brothers didn't see you, so you were never here,' Adam told the farmer once they were back at the farm and mounting the horses ready to return. 'If questioned, you were asleep all night.'

'I was that,' agreed Farmer Starling

cheerfully. 'God speed, sir. And you, Miss Jenny.'

'Adam,' said Jenny in a careful voice, 'not that it isn't wonderful to see the children, but why did you bring the whole family to rescue me?'

Adam shrugged, lighter of heart than he would have believed possible at the start of the evening. 'Ah, well, apart from needing Will to show me the way and Lottie refusing to be left behind, it occurred to me that if I killed your cousin, we'd need to make tracks for the continent. Couldn't leave them behind, could we?'

'A planner to the end,' she said, smiling at him in the pale moonlight.

He smiled back. 'Take my coat. You'll freeze. Did you not have a shawl when they abducted you?'

'I turned it into string. I should have known my smug boast to Lottie some time ago about it being the nicest one I'd ever made would call forth a judgement. I unravelled it and finger-chained the wool to make a thicker strand, then finger-chained that again. It reduces the length dreadfully, but many strands make enough strength to bind a man's hands for a short space.' She turned her face to his, her eyes brilliant with something that made him feel a dozen miles tall. 'It was only to give me something to do. I knew I wouldn't really need it.'

19

It was dawn by the time they were back in the yard of the Bushel. A sleepy stable boy took the horses and a coin to keep quiet about their arrival. Jenny fell into bed beside Lottie, grateful beyond measure to be able to rest safely at last.

Safe. That was the first thought to fill her mind when she struggled to consciousness some hours later in the comparative softness of the inn bed. Beside her, Lottie still slumbered, but when she turned her head, she saw Adam, sitting in the chair on the other side of the room, pulling his boots on and trying to be quiet.

In that moment, she knew that whether Cousin Vincent was convicted or not, whether she could go back and dwell in peace at the Prior's House or not, the one thing she could not do was live without this man.

'Thank you for rescuing me,' she said. 'I don't believe I said it last night.'

'I couldn't not have done,' he replied simply. 'Jenny, we will talk, I promise, but not now. Do you feel able to get up? I must go to the theatre and I would have you safe with us there. Your cousin knows where you are now, but however vengeful he is, he cannot snatch you away in front of a whole company of actors.'

'I can get up. With you in my life, I can do anything,' she said.

He hesitated. 'That, too, we must talk about.'

There was so much pain behind his eyes that Jenny's heart went out to him. 'Adam . . .'

'Later. We have many things to do today. But Jenny, I cannot . . . that is, I am not a suitable . . . ' He shook his head as if it was too full of conflicting thoughts to make sense. 'I will ask the landlady to send up warm water.' With that he left the room.

The first of Adam's 'many things to do' occurred just after ten o'clock when a pounding on the Market Cross stairs nearly made Jenny's heart stop. Three men marched past her on to the stage where the company was rehearsing *Demeter and Persephone*. Lucy stopped halfway through her impassioned speech to Hades, her mouth forming an 'o' of surprise. She blushed as she realised the third man was Mr Browne.

Adam metamorphosed from a glowering, love-struck lord of the underworld into an urbane company manager. 'Good day, gentlemen. The Norwich Company of Comedians, I take it? Allow me to introduce myself. I am Adam Prettyman of the Chartwell Players. I must thank you for the loan of this fine theatre. We do not often play in such splendid surroundings, nor to such a receptive audience as you have nurtured here in Bury St Edmunds. I am happy to inform you of my personal confidence that our new play and accomplished actors will not disgrace either it or you.'

'Blackguard,' said the first of the three men pleasantly. 'How did you persuade the corporation to hire this theatre to you?'

Adam spread his hands. 'Why, we were in the area, and Alderman Taylor having been so kind as to several times commend our playing at Newmarket, when the question of a play for his daughter's birthday was brought up . . .'

The men conferred in furious mutters. It was noticeable to Jenny that young Mr Browne kept breaking off to exchange agonised glances with Lucy, standing beautifully frozen with her hands clasped to her breast.

'This one week and no more,' said the first man shortly. 'The Norwich Company have invested a great deal in the town and the theatre here. We do not appreciate poachers in this part of the country.'

Adam swept him a stage bow. 'You are most kind. Perhaps you would care to watch the bill of fare tonight to ensure the plays put on here are up to your own high standards. *Twelfth Night*, followed by our new afterpiece, *Demeter and Persephone*, which was so well received on Tuesday. I will leave instructions that you are to have your places gratis. I am persuaded you will find the performances most enlightening.'

The older man nodded. 'I doubt that very much, but I'm obliged to you all the same. Come, Browne.' He saw where the young actor's eyes were locked with Lucy's and rolled his own. 'Come away, damn you. I've listened, haven't I? We'll see them play tonight and have done with this nonsense.'

They clumped off. 'Well, well,' said Adam softly. 'It seems a threat to revenues really will move mountains. Who would have thought it?' He swept a glance around the company, gathering everyone's attention. 'You heard that. The great Norwich Company will be watching our efforts this evening. You will never have a better opportunity to make your mark. All of you are good actors, and you were born for this play. Do it well.'

Lottie frowned up at Jenny. 'I don't

understand. What did the men want?'

Jenny pulled the little girl's gown straight. 'They want us gone from here, lest we find better favour with the townsfolk than they do. But they are also curious about the new play, so we must be as good as we possibly can; then they will not mind lending us the theatre.' All the same, she was puzzled. She could have sworn she'd known what was in Adam's mind when he was writing the play, and it did seem from his way of talking to the cast that he was ready to give up the troupe. But if he didn't also want *her*, then what was he about?

★ ★ ★

Jenny might be safe inside the theatre with the whole company watching the single door that gave ingress from the outside, but knowing the threat her cousin posed, she was increasingly on edge as the morning progressed. Just one day back with the earl had reminded her in throat-drying detail how dangerous he was and how inhuman he could be. He would have been so enraged when he discovered she'd escaped that she wondered quite seriously if Billy and Chas Bidens still lived. If they did, they would have lost no time in telling him who had helped her to get away. If not . . . well, she prepared a corner of her mind for the discovery of their lifeless bodies amongst the wreckage of her house. When Will and Lottie proposed going out to get food, she wouldn't let them until Adam was free to accompany them. The memory of her cousin's cold eyes as he'd mentioned 'the little girl' would haunt her forever.

She counted the days again. It was Thursday now. They had until Saturday. She could and would stay hidden, but why had Mr Tweedie not arrived yet? She had provided Samuel with sufficient money to take the mail coach, and she could hardly have been plainer to the solicitor on the need for speed in her letter. What was taking him so long? He must have been, if not delighted, then much encouraged that here was evidence of undoubted felony which could be fixed on the earl. And then she ground her teeth, remembering the months of deliberation before she was allowed to use her own money on the repairs to the Prior's House. Perhaps hours really did tick more slowly inside lawyers' chambers.

At three o'clock, however, a most welcome visitor was admitted to the Market Cross.

'Samuel!' said Adam in delight, springing up from a hasty meal. 'Do you have news?'

'Oh Samuel, why are you not still safe in London?' said Jenny at the same time.

The African player ducked his head in a self-deprecating manner. 'Too many people there,' he said. And more seriously, 'No more running away. I can do more good here. A strange thing happened when I arrived at Mr

Tweedie's chambers. I recognised his partner Mr Congreve as the man who won me in that card game and then released me. He had played for me purely as a humanitarian act, having no idea at the time that Mr Rooke traded in slaves. For my part, I never knew his profession, and we parted that same night. It is no one's fault, but if I had not been cowardly and so quick to hide myself away, if I had spoken out before I joined the Chartwell Players, many of my countrymen's lives might have been spared.'

'What's done is done,' said Adam. 'We can only make amends for the past, not play it over. Congreve, did you say? I knew a Congreve once. He was my brother's contemporary at school and visited us one summer. I daresay it is not the same fellow, but the world is a small place when all's said and done.'

'You will see him later. Having met the Earl of Harwood once, and hearing my history now, he insisted on accompanying Mr Tweedie here. They have taken rooms at the Angel Hotel. They have a judge's warrant with them and have brought two Bow Street Runners to enforce it. Mr Tweedie thinks to hire a post chaise to Rooke Hall tomorrow. I shall go with them. At the very least, I can prevent the earl's servants from giving him any aid.'

Tomorrow. Jenny's appetite deserted her. She pushed her plate sideways towards Will, who finished what was on it before she could change her mind. Tomorrow she would be free. And perhaps, once Cousin Vincent was finally on his way to Bow Street, she could have that talk with Adam.

* * *

The main body of the upper room at the Market Cross was filled with benches, with a raised half-gallery all the way around three walls for the gentry, reached by short flights of steps against the wall at either side. A stair outside the building led to a very high gallery for the working poor, but the only way in for everybody else was the single door just in front of the stage.

Tonight, as previous nights, the front of the pit filled rapidly with expectant townsfolk in their best clothes. Keeping watch through a gap in the curtain, Jenny saw the alderman's party pause in front of the stage to let people move out of their way before ascending jovially to the raised seating. Louisa was looking as beautiful as ever, and was attended by her husband Harry Fortune and several of their acquaintance. It gave Jenny a peculiar feeling to be out of sight just a few feet away like this instead of greeting her friends.

'Is that Mr Tweedie?' asked Lottie, peering through the opening below her and effectively jolting her out of her thoughts.

'Where, sweetheart?'

'Over there, look. He is very thin and he is polishing his glasses just like you said.'

Jenny looked across to her left. 'So it

is,' she said. 'Clever you, remembering that. The tall man with him is Mr Congreve, his partner. I daresay he has been brought along to be a witness when they go to arrest my cousin tomorrow.'

It was a sensible move, Jenny reflected. Mr Congreve was considerably younger, fitter and stronger than Mr Tweedie. From something Susanna's husband Kit had said one time, he was also regularly to be found boxing at Jackson's and fencing at the school next door. Mr Tweedie, for all his fussy old-fashioned ways, was no fool.

The theatre was nearly full when there was an altercation from the front.

'Now what's amiss?' muttered Adam with some annoyance, and went out between the curtains.

'I wish for a box on the stage,' said a cold, authoritative voice.

Jenny's heart stuttered. Cousin Vincent! She immediately locked eyes with Samuel Obidah. The African looked as sick as she felt.

'I'm afraid there are no boxes on the stage in this theatre, sir,' came Adam's pleasant, deferential tones, 'but if you would care to ascend the steps, I fancy the raised gallery will afford you an excellent view.'

'Preposterous,' said the Earl of Harwood, and Jenny heard the stamping of booted feet on stairs. 'Move along there. Move along.'

She flew to the slit in the curtain. Cousin Vincent was settling himself with a very bad grace on the right-hand side of the raised seating, just above the entrance door, his left hand fingering the handle of his whip, his right hand checking on something in his greatcoat pocket. The pocket, Jenny knew, where he habitually kept his pistol. Terror seized her. Over on the left side of the room, she saw Mr Congreve sliding down in his seat until he was obscured by the person in front. Mr Tweedie, meanwhile, was trying to catch the eyes of a pair of thick-set men in the pit.

'All our chickens coming home to

roost,' commented Adam, reappearing between the curtains. 'We cannot do anything now. I must welcome the audience and wish Mrs Fortune felicitations on her birthday. Places everyone, please.'

Jenny caught at his arm. 'Adam, he keeps a pistol in that coat pocket. Oh, do take care. He can only be here for one thing. He means to kidnap me again. Or kill me, if that fails.'

'Or indeed kill both of us,' said Adam. He drew a breath, his eyes calculating. 'However, enraged as he undoubtedly is with me for rescuing you, he is unlikely to shoot me in front of two hundred witnesses. We had best make sure they stay around him for the full duration. Remain out of sight, Jenny. Go nowhere alone. I have half an idea. Trust me.'

'Forever,' she said, and slipped backstage.

Twelfth Night was well received, with Mr Jackson as the unfortunate Malvolio drawing sympathy and derision alike from the audience. Alderman Taylor's roars of laughter were heard several times during the comic scenes, and even the Norwich Company actors had apparently been observed displaying unguarded amusement.

'Wait until the afterpiece,' said Adam. 'They won't be able to forgive us for borrowing their theatre fast enough.'

The Chartwell Players took the unusual step of remaining on the apron of the stage during the interval, the better to mingle with their important guests, rather than having the audience invade the greenroom as was customary. The earl remained in his seat, curling his lip at these tactics. He examined every face, watching the company's comings and goings like a hawk, his hand never straying far from his pocket. On the other side of the raised gallery, Mr Tweedie and Mr Congreve were apparently too deep in conversation to pay any attention to Will, handing round advertisements for the following night's plays. Jenny kept Lottie firmly with her behind the backdrop, watching through a spy hole in the painted canvas.

The actors returned to the green-room, the audience resumed their seats, Mr Furnell sang a trio of sea shanties, and the stage was set for *Demeter and Persephone*.

From the start, the Norwich Company actors were busy scribbling on the left-hand side of the gallery.

'They like it,' murmured Adam to Jenny in satisfaction, standing out of sight at the side to observe Mr and Mrs Jackson's scene as Zeus and Demeter. 'See, the manager is forgetting to write anything down.'

'What of my cousin?' asked Jenny.

Adam smiled. 'Watching my every move.'

But the evening was drawing to an inexorable close. Adam returned to the stage to broodingly oversee the Dance of the Underworld. Jenny watched, anxiety rising ever higher in her throat. 'My cousin means to do something, I know it,' she said to Samuel Obidah. 'He is here for me, but threatening

Adam or the children would be an effective lever. I don't see how Adam can take care of all of us.'

'The earl will do nothing in front of the audience. He is not a stupid man. And he will have noticed Mr Tweedie.'

'He has, but he will assume Mr Tweedie has come to talk to me. I think Mr Congreve has contrived to keep his face hidden. That would certainly put Cousin Vincent on his guard, if he recognised him as the man who won you at cards. I wish I knew what to do for the best. Has Mr Tweedie really got enough with your testimony to press for a conviction?'

'He thinks so,' replied Samuel. 'But . . . '

Jenny felt a further stab of worry. 'But?'

'But money carries authority. I have seen your cousin many times bribe his way out of accusations of cruelty in Jamaica when he was merely rich Mr Rooke.'

'This is England, not Jamaica.'

'Where he is now an earl. A peer of the realm.'

Jenny said slowly, 'And thus thinks himself above the law? You could be right. I still incline to the thought that Cousin Vincent is in the audience to taunt us, and once we are outside in the dark he will pick off first Adam and then me. He is a very good shot.'

'Adam was talking to several of the gentlemen in your friend's party during the interval.'

Jenny felt her stomach clench. 'I know. I saw them. He has probably arranged to have Harry Fortune and his friends surround my cousin and detain him until Mr Tweedie can serve his warrant. It would be better done tonight, as they are all here rather than leaving it until tomorrow.'

'Then why are you worried?'

'Because it will take time for Adam to come off stage, through the pass door and up those steps. It will take even longer for Mr Tweedie to push his way across from the far side of the room.

You must know that when Cousin Vincent is maddened, he possesses enormous strength. They will none of them expect that. I am afraid he will easily free himself from Harry and lunge for Adam; then they will grapple and Cousin Vincent will claim the gun went off by accident in the confusion.' *And I cannot let Adam be killed. I cannot.*

I love him.

'Such a turn of events is more than plausible,' said Samuel reluctantly.

Jenny swallowed, wishing he had not agreed with her, but knowing she was right. 'I am more frightened than I have ever been in my life, but I have to stop this. Perhaps if I go out on the stage to distract him? To draw his attention away from Adam?'

'Then Adam will never forgive any of us. I will restrain you myself rather than allow it. And it will not serve, for he knows you are somewhere here. There is no way out apart from the door by the steps.'

Jenny fingered the spare grey silk hoods placed on the costume table for the final scene. 'Very well, he means to kill me whether I hide or run. Consider this. If I do neither, if I walk out onto the stage in full view, it might lull him into false confidence, imagining he has seen through our ploy of distracting him. He will think himself in command of the situation. He will relax. Samuel, my cousin is cold and analytical, but I have seen him lash out without thought when startled or suddenly angered. You must have done too.'

He nodded. 'What of it?'

'We use it. I believe our only chance of success is to jolt him out of whatever he has planned, to force him to give himself away in front of all these witnesses. We have to make him do something he cannot bribe his way out of, though preferably *not* murder.'

The African looked at her for a long moment. 'No more running,' he murmured, and stood straighter. 'I came back to be of use, to save my countrymen. If you can be brave, so can I. What do you have in mind?'

'It is not a good plan, but it does have the necessary element of shock. What troubles me is the circumstance of Cousin Vincent being so devastatingly accurate.' Jenny took a deep breath and lifted her eyes to meet Samuel's dark ones. 'Tell me, how fast can you duck?'

20

Adam had made what preparations he could in the limited time available and in clear sight of the earl, but the audience was so tight-packed it was doubtful whether his friends would be able to help as much as he'd hoped. Now he strode to centre stage for the last scene, surrounded by his hooded, wraithlike court of the dead.

Lucy, as Persephone, reclined artistically on a sumptuously draped couch, silk and satin cushions piled around her, the one pool of colour amidst the gloom.

Behind him, Adam was aware of his court shifting and knew, with an actor's seventh sense, that there were more people on stage than they had rehearsed with. Turning to Lucy, to beseech her once again to eat something lest her beauty ebb away, he saw a tall figure standing silently at the back and realised Samuel Obidah had taken up position as one of the dead. Out of the corner of his eye, he saw an extra female dead sinking to a graceful crouch. Alarm spread along his already taut nerves. What were they about? Why, in the name of all the gods, was Jenny on stage?

★　★　★

Throughout the interplay of Persephone softening towards him, learning to love him and the final triumph of her eating the pomegranate seeds, his court did nothing out of the ordinary. Jenny's cousin, however, was becoming more watchful, his eyes flicking to the exit as if measuring the distance. When Joe Jackson as Hermes burst on to the stage in a clap of Zeus's thunder to rescue Persephone, the earl jumped, his hand half-pulling out his whip, before subsiding back into his chair, his eyes narrowing more than ever. As Adam bargained spiritedly with Hermes to allow his beautiful Persephone to stay in the underworld for one month of the year for every pomegranate seed eaten, a tiny slice of his attention remained on the earl.

The man clearly had no idea he himself was in any jeopardy. Instead he was coldly assessing every member of the company. He identified Jenny with a thin, derisive smile; and if Adam's resolve had been firm before, it hardened even more at the speculative pause when the earl's gaze reached Lottie. Then he looked directly at Adam, and the steel-hard hatred in his eyes was all Adam needed to jump his plan forward in time by a few notches. It was the only way. Dear God, let him not fail.

The play ended with a touching farewell embrace between Hades and Persephone and her promise to return to him in six months' time, before Demeter swept on stage in the colours of summer to reclaim her daughter. As the audience cheered and the cast bowed, Adam came to the front of the stage.

'We are delighted that our playing has found favour with you today. My thanks to the Bury St Edmunds Corporation,' he said, bowing towards Alderman Taylor, 'and the Norwich Company of Comedians — ' He flourished an imaginary hat towards the left-hand side of the audience. ' — for allowing us the use of this fine theatre. Once again, I would like to wish the fair Mrs Fortune many felicitations on her birthday. And by way of an extra divertissement . . . '

Adam had been walking to and fro across the front of the stage apron as he talked, but at this point he took a giant standing leap clear across from the corner to the right-hand steps leading to the raised gallery. 'I am arresting Vincent, Earl of Harwood for the forcible abduction of his cousin, Lady Jane Rooke.'

The audience gasped and rose to their feet as Adam grasped the earl's arms. Behind Louisa Fortune, her husband pushed forward.

'You madman,' snarled the earl, pulling away as much as the limited space on the gallery platform allowed. He was as tense as a strung bow and far, far stronger than Adam had expected. With a sharp twist, his hand came out of his pocket, his fingers curling around a deadly-looking pistol.

Adam cursed frantically. Jenny had been right. He adjusted his hold to grip below Vincent's elbow. How stupid of him to have underestimated his adversary's strength. Adam was taller and stronger than anyone he knew, but the earl was struggling like a man possessed. What was worse, he didn't seem fussy about where the gun was pointing. Adam hung on and listened through the audience's screams for any sound that Mr Tweedie's Bow Street Runners were making their way towards him.

'I have done nothing wrong,' hissed the earl, his face livid. 'You are the one who abducted my cousin from my protection and from the safety of her own house. Your men lie dead there even now. How dare you, a commoner, accuse me? I would be within my rights to shoot you where you stand.'

'Not in England, cousin,' said Jenny's clear voice from the stage. From the audience's reaction, Adam guessed she had pulled off her hood.

Jenny, you brave, glorious, idiotically confident woman. Don't you know I am only barely holding on to your cousin's gun hand? He willed her to stay to one side of the stage, where she would be shielded to some extent by Adam's own body, and not move out to the middle where she would be an easy target.

'To me, Lottie,' she said. 'Just in case one of the earl's bullets should happen to go astray, as I believe must have happened to the men imprisoning me in my house, for they were alive and unpleasantly vociferous when I left. Yes, that's right, get behind my skirts.'

Adam could feel the earl's hatred; he could feel him resisting with whipcord muscles; could feel him trying to provoke a scuffle during which his gun might legitimately go off. Adam was having to exert all his strength to keep the man still, but do it he would, even if he had to break both his arms.

A new authoritative voice sounded from his left — that of Mr Tweedie's partner, who was far more suited to shoulder through the audience than the elderly solicitor. 'Let me by, please. I have a warrant for the arrest of the Earl of Harwood.'

The audience hushed in avid interest at this new development.

'What arrest?' snarled the earl. 'She was on her own land. You are bluffing. I will see you all on the gallows for this.' He struggled in Adam's grip again, almost succeeding in raising his gun.

Sweat stood out on Adam's brow as he bore down on his opponent's hand, trying not to think how much damage a bullet through his leg would do. The man was near inhuman with spleen. Was this what he himself had been like before he learnt to channel his fury? No wonder he had been shunned and feared. No wonder he had been repulsed so comprehensively. The knowledge added another layer of pain. The determination to restrain Vincent Rooke now warred with the old griping sickness in his soul.

'My warrant is not for kidnap,' said Mr Congreve, sounding nearer, but not yet near enough for Adam to relinquish his hold. 'We shall be applying for that once we have received these good people's deputations. The warrant I am serving now relates to your felonious activity of engagement in slave trading, in direct contravention of His Majesty's laws.'

Vincent laughed, a high-pitched sound that shivered the souls of all who heard him. 'Ridiculous. I am the Earl of Harwood. I have nothing to fear from your ludicrous accusations.'

'Now,' Adam heard Jenny say quietly.

'Nothing to fear, Vincent Rooke?' came a slow, rich voice, pitched to reverberate around the whole theatre.

'Nothing to fear? Not even with the sworn eye-witness testimony of a free man to give you the lie?'

There was another gasp from the audience. It was Samuel Obidah who had spoken. From the sound of it, the actor was standing squarely in the centre of the stage and must also have taken off his hood. Adam hoped to God no one was near him.

For a single, rigid moment, the earl seemed paralysed with shock. Then he let out a feral scream and, in the split second when Adam's hold faltered, jerked his hand up and fired at the stage just as Jenny yelled, 'Down!'

Adam regained his grip, shook the gun out of Vincent's hand, and caught his wrists behind his back. Harry Fortune shoved forward the last few steps to help overpower him. Then the two burly Bow St Runners clumped ponderously up the steps to take proceedings from there.

'Oh, well done, Mr Prettyman, well done indeed.' Mr Tweedie had managed to reach them and was bobbing up and down, wreathed in smiles. 'All witnessed, Mr Congreve, and attempted murder too. That's fourteen years transportation at the very least.'

Harry Fortune clapped him on the back. 'Magnificent show, Prettyman.'

Amidst the buffets and congratulations, Adam turned and looked at the stage. There was a bullet hole ripped in the backcloth about the height of a man's heart. Samuel was just rising from the boards and dusting himself down. Jenny had one arm around Lottie and the other on Will's shoulder. Her gaze was full of pride and her eyes were fixed on Adam's face. Her absolute, unquestioning confidence in him was unbearable.

21

Over. It was over. Relief pounded Jenny from all sides, but she seemed unable to take it in. Her attention was centred solely on Adam. Her cousin was hauled away by the Runners, struggling and blaspheming, with spittle trickling from the corner of his mouth. She saw Adam turn, dazed as much from the shock of the gun going off by his ear as by the sudden lack of need to hang on any longer to a madman. He had done that for her, risked that appalling jump and tackled Vincent, knowing he was armed, for *her*. She was so, so proud of him.

'Wonderful,' she mouthed. But before she could do or say more, he was surrounded by well-wishers, buffeting him on the back, clouting him on the shoulder and generally heaping congratulations on him.

Louisa Fortune had broken away

from her party to run to her friend, and now paused comically at the top of the steps. 'But how do I reach you?' she called to Jenny.

'We go around, my love,' said her husband with a laugh, wrapping one arm around her waist to guide her down the stairs. 'Unless you too can leap six-foot gaps with a single bound. Sweetest jump I ever saw, Prettyman, but I'm blowed if I know how you did it.'

Jenny saw Adam measure the gap with his eyes. He looked a little sick. 'I had to,' he said to Harry. 'It was the only way the element of surprise would work. I wouldn't take odds on my being able to do it again.'

The theatre emptied as, with the evening's entertainment apparently finished, the audience reluctantly left and those most concerned joined Jenny and the company on the stage. She wanted to fly to Adam, to wrap her arms around him; but no sooner was he free of the congratulatory buffets than he was snagged by the Norwich manager and was now being talked to with much earnestness and significant looks towards the players. Ale and wine and pastries appeared ('The alderman sent out for them,' reported Will with his mouth full) and the atmosphere grew jovial. Jenny ate and drank a little, and tried to concentrate on what Mr Tweedie was telling her about trustees and settlements and *loco parentis*, but found herself swaying and the lamps flickering.

'Darling Jenny, you must and shall come home with us,' declared Louisa.

Lottie gasped and clutched Jenny's skirt, waking her most effectively.

'Dearest Louisa,' she replied with a smile, 'you are always so kind, but I have a perfectly good room at the inn which, moreover, I have already paid for, as the landlady mistrusts actors not to skip away in the early dawn. Indeed, I think Lottie and I at any rate should be going back there very soon, for neither of us got much sleep last night.'

Lottie obligingly yawned and leaned against Jenny's leg. Jenny looked up and caught Adam's eye. He nodded and began to bring the conversation with the Norwich man to a close.

Louisa's bright gaze had followed the tiny exchange. 'Oh,' she said with an air of enlightenment. 'Oh, I see. Well, I daresay we will get together soon enough for a proper talk.' She leaned forward to breathe in Jenny's ear. 'Prodigiously athletic. I am very pleased for you. But do let Mr Tweedie manage the settlements, won't you?'

Jenny felt her colour rise. 'I will call on you very soon, Louisa, I promise. Now, if you love me, do pray leave and take everyone with you.'

★ ★ ★

Even while he was discussing the wholesale transfer of the Chartwell Players to the Norwich Company of Comedians, Adam was aware of Jenny on the other side of the stage. She held herself for all the world as if she were at an evening soirée, smiling and talking politely to her friends though she must be near asleep on her feet. Just as when they had called on Alderman Taylor, seeing her now with Louisa Fortune reminded him anew of her proper status. He ached with wanting her, and was burning his boats comprehensively with regard to the company, but how could they ever deal together? Then he heard Louisa laughingly declare that Jenny must go back with them, and lost the thread of his own conversation in the silence of his heart. But Jenny was smiling and shaking her head, then she looked at him with 'May we *please* depart now?' in her eyes, and he heard his heartbeat again, reassuring and steady.

He nodded to the Norwich man and told him he'd speak to the company. Then he gathered the Players' attention and made packing up motions. He glanced at Jenny again. She smiled and bent to say something to Lottie. Adam's heart stirred once more. It was nearly the same wordless communication he and Mary had had, but not quite. He must not give in to its allure.

'Are you all right?' he asked in a low voice as they loaded the wagon.

She nodded. 'I'm just tired.'

They started back to the inn in silence, Lottie perched next to Will, who was driving the wagon. The rhythmic clopping of the horses' hooves in the quiet night air soothed Adam. Jenny's weight on his arm felt exactly right — and bittersweet.

Behind them, he could hear the second wagon and the murmur of conversation. He suspected the others were discussing him and his actions, and he knew he would have to put the Norwich Company's offer to the troupe, but not yet, not tonight. His head was too crowded with all that had happened this evening. He did not believe any of the players would object to exchanging their respectable-but-makeshift touring life for the much more prestigious Outer Circuit, but he still needed a period of adjustment and considered reflection before acquainting them with the proposal. Just now, he didn't have the words. They simply weren't there and he was finding that difficult to grasp. It was so odd not to have the company and its business filling the larger part of his consciousness. The Chartwell Players had been his life for over ten years, but its dissolution was currently far from foremost in his thoughts. Ever since he had received Jenny's note yesterday, there had been no one else in his mind but her.

'It seems strange,' remarked Jenny, unconsciously echoing his feelings, 'not to be worrying about my cousin any longer. I don't think I have been this free of anxiety since before my father died. My mind cannot quite encompass the change. At what time did you arrange for us to call on Mr Tweedie tomorrow?'

'I said we would be at the theatre around ten of the clock. I am at your service to accompany you to the Angel Hotel, but there will be no need for him to see me.'

'What nonsense. Mr Tweedie will want to thank you in elaborate formal language on behalf of the estate, and to be perfectly truthful, there were things he was saying this evening that I did not take in at all. I would be grateful for your presence and the loan of your memory when I see him next.'

'He will explain them again, I am sure. You are safe now, Jenny. You do not need me.' His voice almost broke on the words, but he managed to hold it together. Who would have thought his acting ability would break his heart?

'Adam, for an intelligent, forward-thinking man, you are occasionally very blind. Do you not yet know that I will *always* need you?'

His heart twisted and he turned his face away from her. 'Jenny, I am no good to you. I am no good to any woman. There is the inn ahead. I will unload and help Will with the horses. You had best get yourself and Lottie to bed.'

She looked at him for a long moment. 'I love you, Adam.'

He almost doubled up with the pain of hearing her words and not being able to return them. 'You cannot,' he said bleakly. 'You do not know what I am.'

★   ★   ★

Thoughts hurried through Jenny's head as she readied Lottie for bed. It was not the rejection of her love that occupied her, for she knew in a thousand ways that Adam reciprocated it. It was his denial that she must address, and soon. Now was not the time to ask Adam if *he* needed *her*. Now was not the time to point out that his daughter already felt the want of a mother and that both his children had stolen her heart. It wasn't even the time to say that his earlier words were wrong, that Jenny would never now be able to live without him. This, right now, tonight, was the moment to heal Adam of his past.

Accordingly, once Lottie was snuggled down and Will appeared, yawning mightily and saying everyone was back and Pa was seeing to something or other with the wagons, she laid down her sewing and wrapped her Norwich shawl snugly about her shoulders. 'Then I shall go down and talk to him there,' she said. She caught Lottie's quick look of alarm. 'Goose,' she said, giving the child a kiss. 'I shall be back directly. If you can leave me a little of the bed to sleep in, I would appreciate it.'

She found Adam in the barn, standing by one of the wagons with his back to her and his forehead pillowed on his arms in the attitude of a man with very nearly too much to bear. Her heart went out to him.

'Why?' she said. 'Why are you no good to any woman? From what I have witnessed first hand these past weeks, I can think of very few people better.'

He did not look at her, but she saw the red suffusing his neck. 'Jenny, you should not be here. I am best left alone when I have the black dog on me.'

She walked up to him and laid a hand on his forearm. 'Then you must become accustomed to having a limpet, for I am not letting you go until you tell me what is wrong.'

He flung her off with a groan. 'Go, Jenny. I am not fit for you. Trust me, you do not want to know what I have been. And I do not want to talk about it.'

Jenny sat composedly on one of the crates which had been unloaded because it was not necessary this week. 'I may not know what you have been in the past, but I know what you are now. You are honourable, principled, a good manager, a good father, strong, honest . . .'

'Flawed. Selfish. Hot-tempered.'

She smiled and patted the crate beside her. 'Loyal. Stubborn . . .'

He sat reluctantly. 'Undependable . . .'

'Incomplete.'

'Stop it, Jenny. You are destroying me.'

'That is odd, for my intention is entirely the opposite. Adam, I love you. I will love you until the end of time. So will you please tell me why you are not offering for me this very minute? It cannot be that you are fighting shy of all the work there is still to do on the Prior's House.'

He turned to her. 'It is not that at all, you impossible woman.'

Jenny took both his hands. 'Then tell me what it is. You cannot keep this inside you any longer. You need to let it out, let the air in.'

'I cannot offer for you. I am flawed. Have you never seen a tree with a canker at its heart? That is me. Sound enough on the outside, but out of a clear sky the tree will split apart and destroy all around it.'

'It did not today, and I thought you were tried pretty hard. Talk, Adam. I am not letting go of you until you do.'

'I cannot,' he ground out. 'I do not want to lose your good opinion.'

Jenny smiled. 'Then I do matter to you.'

He met her eyes. 'How can you doubt it?'

Still holding on to his hands, Jenny shifted closer to him and rested her head against his chest. 'This is where I belong. Here, with you. In a barn, on the road, in a crumbling house with great splintered holes in half the floors and very likely the rest of it destroyed in a fit of temper. You know it and I know it. Talk to me, Adam. Cut the canker away. It is *not*, for example, that you think we will be an unequal match, so do not even think of gammoning me that it is.'

Adam loosened one hand and put his arm around her. As soon as he did, Jenny felt him relax, as if the unconditional, casual, non-alarming contact was what he needed. 'No,' he said on a sigh. 'I cannot boast an earl in the family, but I am a gentleman's son. A gentleman's third son, to be exact. How did you guess?'

'You have a natural presence. And you were by far too knowledgeable about estate matters not to have been born to the land somewhere.'

'My father is a local squire in Staffordshire. My eldest brother married well enough and lives at the manor with his family, ready to take over the reins from my father just as soon as he's allowed. My middle brother is with the army. I had no taste for fighting or the sea, no leaning towards the church, and I was not thought promising enough for the universities, so I worked with our steward on the estate. I received an allowance from the family, but there was never enough to spare for more, and I gradually realised that I was *expected* to stay and work, virtually for free, for the good of the family and the estate. I didn't mind much, because it was all I had ever known, until . . . until . . . '

Jenny held his hand more securely. 'Until?'

He took a deep breath. 'Until the younger sister of my brother's wife came to us for a long visit. I was eighteen, ripe for falling in love, and Chloe was so very beautiful.'

'Ah,' said Jenny.

Adam slanted a look down at her. 'Indeed. Looking back now, I realise she was just as innocent as I was, or maybe not quite so, for she surely knew she was there to be found a husband from the surrounding Staffordshire gentry.'

'It is,' said Jenny with feeling, 'the fate of all young marriageable ladies who do not have parents of sufficient calibre to resist society.'

He gave a short laugh. 'Chloe hadn't the remotest inclination to resist. She wanted to be wooed, wanted to fall deliciously in love and have settlements and be looked after. And I was in the house, and young and admiring and impassioned, and she was fluttery and flattered and naively happy in a biddable, unworldly way.'

'Oh, Adam.' Jenny squeezed his hand in sympathy.

He gave a short laugh. 'Just so. There was to be a ball at the largest house in the district, to which we were all invited. I was ready before the rest, and when Chloe came downstairs she was so lovely that I offered for her there and then. My sister-in-law was horrified.

She lost no time in telling me that she had *much* grander plans for Chloe. She had the son of our titled neighbour in her sights, no less. Indeed, I was informed in no uncertain terms by her, my brother and even by my father that with no prospects, I would never be thought a good enough match for any young woman, let alone a beauty like Chloe.'

'How needlessly cruel,' cried Jenny indignantly. 'How dare they be as mean as that when you had never been given indications as to your future.'

'It was a body blow such as I had never previously received. You will have noticed I have a temper. I kept it in check at first, for I was too shocked to be angry, but the injustice grew in me during the evening. At the ball, it sickened me beyond measure that Chloe was near enough served up on a platter for Lord Stephen. I admit freely that I had never liked him; and that night, from general gossip and what I saw with my own eyes, he had at least one mistress present, maybe two. You may imagine how I felt, thinking of him marrying my Chloe.

Halfway through the evening, I noticed him drawing Chloe outside. She glanced anxiously at my sister-in-law, who pretended not to see. I was very sore of heart by then, so in a glowering, sulky, brooding fashion I followed them, not intending anything but to make myself more miserable. As soon as they were hidden from the terrace, Lord Stephen had his hand inside Chloe's bodice and his disgusting, licentious tongue down her throat. He'd never had any intention of offering for her!

I saw red. I waded in with both fists flying and a yell the Scots would have been proud of at Culloden. By the time my friends pulled me off him, I'd half-killed the man. I'd be surprised if he can use his wedding tackle to this day.'

Jenny chuckled. 'I cannot say I blame you, and I imagine Chloe was extraordinarily thankful, but I don't suppose it went down at all well with the neighbourhood.'

'Chloe,' said Adam in a clipped voice, 'was terrified. She shrank away from me. I was too big, too rough, and I had scared her. I had misled her with my false talk of poetry and books. She was, of course, very grateful to have been rescued. But fighting was of all things the most barbaric, and she would never be able to look on me in the same light again.'

'What a goose,' said Jenny prosaically. 'She wouldn't have made you happy. Please tell me she didn't marry Lord Stephen?'

Adam let out a long sigh. 'She married a well-to-do widower with a grown-up family. He doted on her and bought her everything she expressed a passing fancy for. I left the morning after the wedding. I was too heartsick and humiliated to stay. I'd always had a hankering for the theatre after enjoying the local touring company's visits, so I decided to try striking out for myself as an actor.'

'Which you did, and for which, incidentally, I am extremely grateful. Adam, the thought of you half-killing a rake doesn't disgust me.'

'But the animal inside me would,' he said in a low, ashamed tone. 'Just as it did Chloe. I lost control several times in those early days before I learnt how to channel the rage.'

'You were very young, big for your years, sheltered, and still hurting. I can see why you might hit out when provoked. But you are not that boy anymore. You *did* learn to control your anger. You have nothing to be ashamed of. Listen to me, Adam. Did you ever scare Mary?'

'No, but . . . Mary was older. She was smarting like me when we met, but with her it was because she was not allowed to practise medicine. She wanted to get away. She wanted to take control of her life. Ours was a partnership as much as a love match, though I didn't realise it until she was close to death. And then I was angry again because she had allowed me to fail her. I cannot be trusted, Jenny.'

'Foolish man. I trust you. I have trusted you since the moment I stepped through the door of the barn in Clare when I knew nothing of you, bar that you were several times kind to Susanna, and that you needed a bookkeeper. Since then, you have shielded me, looked after me, listened to me, believed me. You have let me help you, you have let me help your children. You have saved me from drowning, you have rescued me from abduction. Tonight alone you saved three lives — mine, Lottie's and Samuel's.' She put a hand up to touch the side of his face. 'How can I not love you, Adam?'

For a moment, the world was held in the balance; but then she lifted her face to his and at last, at last, at last his mouth came down to meet hers.

22

The Prior's Ground: April 1818

Jenny felt herself lifted from the carriage, felt Lottie scramble down beside her, heard Will gently whispering to the horses to bide where they were.

Then Adam set her feet down on a newly gravelled sweep and his gentle, loving hands untied her mask strings.

'Behold, Mrs Prettyman, the Prior's House is restored.'

Jenny smiled up at her husband. 'I know that. It is what we have been working towards all these last months.'

Lottie danced in excitement beside her. 'But now it is *finished*, Jenny-Mama, even if we are not to live in it yet.'

'I would like to live here,' said Eddie from where he was seated at the front of the carriage next to Will. 'It is friendlier than Rooke Hall.'

Jenny smiled at her young cousin. 'It is smaller, certainly. But Rooke is your home, Eddie, which is why we keep you company there. When you are grown up, you will marry and have a family of your own to fill it and stop you from being lonely. Meanwhile, Adam teaches you to look after your estate, and I keep all the accounts straight for you.'

'And we play in all the passages and all the rooms to stop them getting sad and dusty,' laughed Lottie.

And no one would ever fear Eddie's father again, for despite appeals and solicitors and a shocking amount of money changing hands, last month a jury of his peers had found him guilty of the murder of illegal slaves, and his shade no longer troubled the earth.

Lottie held Eddie's hand as they ran ahead into the Prior's House, though by now the children were all as familiar with it as Jenny was herself. Will drove the carriage around to the stable yard. Jenny and Adam followed more slowly.

'Do you mind?' asked Adam.

Jenny took his arm to help her unwieldy body up the low step to the front door. 'Mind not living here? A little, yes, but how could we not take charge of Rooke and Eddie when the trustees asked us to? Will and Lottie do not mind where we live as long as Will has his horses and Lottie has all of us close by. Samuel and Ruth have gone back to Jamaica to run the plantation humanely. You and I have fifteen or sixteen years to turn Eddie into a fine young man who will treat Rooke well and rid the estate of his father's evil taint, brief though it was. And then . . . '

'And then we will have the rest of our lives together here. I love you very much, Jenny. Mary was my rudder when I needed one, and I will always be grateful for her belief in me and for the gift of our children.' He stopped and took Jenny in his arms. 'But you are my anchor and, paradoxically, you are also the wind that set me free. As soon as I saw you I knew I had come home.'

'Even if you did resist it for the longest time. Adam, I love you very much too, and I could live in your kisses forever. But if you hold me that tight, you will start off our next adventure before our little one is quite ready for it. I do not object *exactly* to the heir of the Prior's Ground being born on the premises, but all things considered, I would rather wait until Susanna and Kit and their family arrive next week and the children are occupied elsewhere instead of being interested spectators at the event.'

Adam smiled lovingly at her. 'Then I shall unhand you with reluctance, and we will go and partake of a surprise picnic meal in the dining room, which I believe I can hear the children have now smuggled in via the side door.'

Love and warmth and sheer, unbounded happiness filled Jenny. 'I didn't say you had to unhand me,' she murmured. 'Simply not hold me quite so tightly. I daresay they would appreciate a few more minutes to spread the cloth and set the plates out. Not to mention sufficient time to sample the wares to make sure cook has put in the correct pies and buns.'

'Wise as ever, my love. One should never hurry children.'

No, thought Jenny as their lips met in a slow, magical embrace every bit as good as the one on their wedding night, *I remember*.

Acknowledgements

Any mistakes are my own, but I owe particular thanks to

Newmarket library, for the wealth of local interest books and documents on their shelves

The Newmarket Local History Society, for access to research material

Colin Blumenau for putting on so many wonderful Georgian productions while he was artistic director at The Theatre Royal, Bury St Edmunds

The wonderful (and very talented) Louise Allen for correcting my historical gaffes and for having laws-of-arrest knowledge at her fingertips

Jane Dixon-Smith for exactly the right cover, once again

and you, if I've forgotten to include you

We do hope that you have enjoyed reading this large print book.

Did you know that all of our titles are available for purchase?

We publish a wide range of high quality large print books including:
Romances, Mysteries, Classics
General Fiction
Non Fiction and Westerns

Special interest titles available in large print are:
The Little Oxford Dictionary
Music Book, Song Book
Hymn Book, Service Book

Also available from us courtesy of Oxford University Press:
Young Readers' Dictionary
(large print edition)
Young Readers' Thesaurus
(large print edition)

For further information or a free brochure, please contact us at:
Ulverscroft Large Print Books Ltd.,
The Green, Bradgate Road, Anstey,
Leicester, LE7 7FU, England.
Tel: (00 44) 0116 236 4325
Fax: (00 44) 0116 234 0205

Other titles in the
Linford Romance Library:

DESIGN FOR LOVE

Ginny Swart

With her promotion to assistant art director at Market Media, a lovely new flat, and her handsome steady boyfriend Grant, Andrea Ross's future looks rosy. But when her gentle, fatherly boss decides to retire, and the company hires Luke Sullivan as the new art director, nothing is certain anymore. With a reputation as both a slave driver and a serial charmer of women, he quickly stamps his imprint on the department. Meanwhile, things with Grant aren't exactly going to plan . . .

THE SIGNET RING

Anne Holman

Resigned to spinsterhood, Amy Gibbon is astounded to receive a proposal of marriage from Viscount Charles Chard upon their very first meeting! Love quickly flares in her heart, but Charles is more reticent — he needs an heir, and this is a marriage of convenience. Determined to win her new husband over, Amy follows him to France amid the dangers of the Napoleonic wars, where he must search for his father's precious stolen signet ring. Can true love blossom under such circumstances?

THE LOST YEARS

Irena Nieslony

Upon returning from their honey-moon in Tanzania, Eve Masters and her new husband David are quickly embroiled in chaos. When a hit-and-run accident almost kills them both, David develops amnesia and has no recollection of who Eve is. And then she pays a visit to his first wife — to find her dead body slumped over the kitchen table, with herself as the prime murder suspect! Will Eve be able to solve this tangled web, and will David remember her again — or will the villains win for the first time?

SAFE HAVEN

Eileen Knowles

Taking shelter from a snowstorm, Giselle Warren revisits an isolated holiday cottage, expecting it to be vacant — and walks straight into someone's home instead! Blake Conrad, the owner, has moved in after splitting with his girlfriend. In rocky circumstances of her own with her fiancé, who she suspects wants to marry her purely for her money, Giselle has been hoping for solitude in which to gather her thoughts. But this chance meeting with Blake will change both of their lives forever — after she makes him an incredible proposition . . .

A TOUCH OF THE EXOTIC

Dawn Knox

From India to war-torn London to an estate in Essex, Samira's life is one of rootlessness and unpredictability. With her half-Indian heritage, wherever she goes she's seen as 'exotic', never quite fitting in despite her best efforts. To add to her troubles, her beauty attracts attention from men that she's not sure how to handle. But when she falls for handsome RAF pilot Luke, none of her charms seem to work, as it appears his heart is already bestowed elsewhere . . .